JENNIFER HAYDEN

SMOKESCREEN

JENNIFER HAYDEN

SMOKESCREEN

ISBN: 9798362964528

1

When Mila Barnes turned eight years old, her teacher asked her what she wanted to be when she grew up. She had one answer.

A police officer.

That answer didn't change as she went through school. While she took a slight detour after graduation and enlisted in the army, her career aspirations didn't alter.

Upon fulfilling her requirement, she came back to Oregon — to Eugene, where she'd grown up — and signed on with the police department.

At twenty-six years old, she'd been a rookie cop. She'd been partnered almost immediately with a chauvinistic, lazy egomaniac named Jeff Winters. They'd butted heads almost from the get-go. He liked flexing his muscles — letting her know he had the upper hand and two more years of experience on the force than she did. He was good at dictating, but bad at follow-through. Regardless, she'd learned to navigate her daily routine with him, even though she'd hated every minute of it.

And then he'd been promoted.

Initially, she'd been ecstatic. She no longer had to deal with his pompous, obnoxious inuendo and ridicule.

Her relief had been short-lived. Even as a detective, it seemed Winters continued to stand in her way. She was a good cop, had good instincts. She knew it. But he just refused to take her seriously. And somehow, no matter what situation she encountered, it always seemed she was answering to him.

So she'd quit.

Just like that, she'd walked away from her dream, packed her things and headed up north.

Portland was a big city. Their police bureau needed people, just like most departments across the country did currently.

Sammy Haynes, a detective already on the payroll in Portland, had put in a good word for her. They'd recently crossed paths professionally when she'd helped him on a case he'd been working.

Sammy was one of the good guys. The moment she'd met him, she'd seen the determination in his eyes—the honesty. He was a genuine, hardworking cop, who gave his job the 100% he felt it deserved. He was the kind of cop she strived to be.

Now, as she stood in her new apartment amidst packing boxes and the chaos that came with a move as unplanned as this one was, she exhaled painfully and gave herself a peptalk.

"This is what you wanted," she muttered, raking a hand through her shoulder length, auburn locks. "Starting fresh is a good thing. You made the right decision."

The words echoed throughout the empty room. Reaching for a packing box, she began to unpack her kitchen utensils.

The apartment was on the second floor of an old Victorian in the heart of Portland. She had Sammy Haynes to thank for it, too. He'd recommended the place to her. His girlfriend, Jacy Colson, had a brother who lived in the apartment downstairs. Liam Colson had a daughter and had just gone through a tough divorce. Another brother, Drew, also a cop, had a girlfriend who'd lived in this unit until the two had decided to move in together recently.

The apartment had one bedroom. It was freshly painted and everything was clean and shiny. The rent was right and the neighborhood was decent. It felt like another piece to her puzzle fitting right into place.

Hearing her phone ring, she reached for her pocket where she usually kept the device. Upon checking the ID, she saw her brother was calling.

Reid Barnes had always been her biggest supporter. Four years older than she was, he, too, had done a stint in the army. He currently lived in Washington State near Mt. Rainier, where he was a higher-ranking member of the search and rescue team there.

Giving up on the boxes that surrounded her, she shoved one aside and took a seat on the nearby couch as she answered the call. "What's up, big brother?"

"Not much. Just checking in. How's the unpacking?"

"Terrible. I got rid of a bunch of stuff in Eugene and I still have too much crap."

He chuckled. "Start by eliminating half the boxes that are marked *closet*."

They'd always had a running joke about the amount of clothing she had. Even as a kid she'd been addicted to fashion. "I was thinking about starting with the boxes marked *kitchen*." She'd never been much of a cook.

"You have to eat, kid."

She tended to eat out a lot. Leaning back

against the cushions of her leather couch, she sighed. "Who am I to put McDonald's out of business?"

He chuckled again. "I suppose you've got me there. So when do you start work?"

"Monday." She was counting the minutes. She was excited to get back on the job.

"You going to be ready by then? This was a big move."

"I'll be unpacking for the next two months at least. I don't have the unreasonable expectation of finishing before I start work."

"I can take a few days off—come help, if you need me."

She knew her brother was busy as hell himself. "I'll be fine, Reid."

"You made this decision awfully quickly. I know you were having some problems in Eugene but—"

"This isn't as sudden as you think. I was unhappy in Eugene for a long time. I was trying to make it work." She stared up at the ceiling. "I kept thinking there was a promotion for me around the corner."

"There might have been," he replied quietly.

"Even if there was, it wouldn't have been worth it. I can't work with Winters."

"That asshole needs to be fired. Did you file a complaint when you left?"

She'd wanted to. But she hadn't. She knew she wanted to continue her career in law enforcement and leaving a department with a black mark on her record didn't seem like a good idea. Bitchers and complainers were never well-received, legitimate or not. "I didn't want the negative attention. I'm starting fresh. That's enough."

He mumbled under his breath.

"It is what it is, Reid. Just let it go. I have."

She knew him well enough to suspect he wanted to argue but he didn't. "Whatever you say. I'm going to find some time and head down that way soon. Be ready."

"Why do you make that sound so ominous?"

"I'm not trying to. Just fair warning."

Reid had always been over-protective. Fluent in Karate, he'd taught her every form of self-defense he knew the minute she'd turned twelve. He'd also made sure she was well aware of the fact that men were pigs and she needed to watch out for herself. Their father had died of a heart attack just before her tenth birthday. From that moment on, Reid had stepped in and taken over as the male role model in her life. She couldn't help but appreciate the fact that he cared so much.

"You need to spend less time worrying about me." She straightened and dangled one hand between her knees. "You know I can take care of myself."

"I know it. You're in a new place though. Portland can be rough in areas."

"Eugene isn't exactly Eutopia."

"Maybe not but you grew up there."

Before she could reply there was a knock on the front door. A little startled, she climbed to her feet.

"What's that noise?" he asked.

She crossed to the door. "Someone just knocked on my door."

"Who would be knocking on your door?"

She was wondering the same thing. When she peered through the peephole, she didn't see anyone right away. Not until she lowered her gaze. That's when she noticed a small child standing on the welcome mat she'd laid in front of the door mere hours earlier. "I've got to go," she said to her brother. "I'll call you later." She disconnected before he could argue and opened the door.

Now that there wasn't a barrier between them, Mila could see the little girl more clearly. She was tiny, with a dark mop of curls that haphazardly framed her cherubic face. She was wearing bright pink jeans and a T-shirt, a pair of white Converse sneakers on her feet. Her eyes were round and gray as they stared up into

Mila's face curiously. "Who are you?"

The question caught her off guard and Mila frowned. Leaning against the doorjamb, she folded her arms over her chest. "Mila. More importantly, who are *you*?"

"I'm not supposed to talk to strangers."

Mila found herself biting back a smile. "Yet, here you are."

The little girl bit her bottom lip. "I'm looking for Amber. She's my uncle's girlfriend. She's tall and blond and really pretty. Do you know her?"

"No, I can't say that I do." A thought occurred to her. "You wouldn't be Shaylee, would you?"

The little girl's eyes grew wide. "You know my name?"

This time Mila outright smiled. "I've met your uncles."

Shaylee smiled herself and exposed a gap where one of her front teeth had once been. "Both of them?"

"Yes. I'm a police officer, just like they are."

"You're a lady cop? Like Finley is?"

"I don't know who Finley is."

"She works at the police station with my uncles. She gives me suckers when I go there. She's pretty with dark hair and brown eyes. Kind of like you."

Mila instantly liked this kid. She was cute as

a button. "Thank you."

"You're welcome. Can I come in?"

Her instincts kicking in, Mila hesitated. "Are you supposed to be up here by yourself?"

Shaylee tapped her sneaker against the welcome mat and shoved her hands into the pockets of her pants. "My dad is making dinner."

That didn't exactly answer Mila's question. Before she could say anything more, she heard footsteps on the stairs behind the child.

"Shaylee!" a male voice called.

Shaylee stiffened and turned toward the voice just as its owner hit the top of the stairs.

Since Mila had met both Drew and Slade Colson, she'd figured out they were identical in just about every way physically. Sammy had informed her at some point that they were two of a set of triplets. The man standing before her currently was obviously the remaining third of their equation.

Just like his brothers, he was tall with dark hair and gray eyes. She noted right away that his hair was shorter. His face was spackled with a good layer of dark stubble. He was dressed casually, in jeans and a black T-shirt, a scuffed-up pair of boots on his feet.

At the moment, he looked a bit on the annoyed side. "Shaylee Elizabeth, what did I tell you about leaving the apartment without asking?"

"But I just came up here to see Amber, Daddy."

He continued to frown. "I explained to you that Amber moved in with Uncle Drew. She doesn't live up here anymore."

Shaylee's bottom lip pooched out. "I forgot."

Immediately the man's frown thinned out and his expression softened. "Even if she did still live up here, it's not okay for you to wander off by yourself. We've been over this."

"I'm sorry, Daddy. I won't do it again." She smiled from ear to ear. "I met Mila." She gestured to Mila happily.

For the first time, the man's eyes lifted and locked with Mila's.

"Mila Barnes," she said quietly, offering him her hand.

He automatically reciprocated with his own. "Liam Colson. I live downstairs."

"I know. I've met both your brothers."

He stared at her for a long moment. "Yeah, they mentioned you." He backed up a little sheepishly. "I would have come up and introduced myself but I've been on shift. Fire department. My schedule's a little erratic."

"I work nights, too. Or I will anyway, when I start on Monday." One of the concessions she'd had to make was a change from day to night shift. That's what being the low person on the totem pole got you.

"Good to know," he said, folding his arms over his chest. "You moved from Eugene, right?"

She nodded.

"Daddy, can Mila come and eat dinner with us? I want to introduce her to Lucky."

Liam hissed out a breath, obviously uncomfortable.

If Mila hadn't felt a little put on the spot herself, she would have laughed. Instead, she gave the child her full attention. "Who is Lucky?"

"My kitty. Uncle Drew gave him to me. He's brown and white with little gold spots on his belly. He's good luck."

Shaylee's expression was so serious Mila couldn't help but grin in return. "He sounds really neat."

Liam was still standing there silently, apparently unsure what to say to get himself out of the awkward situation.

Deciding to show mercy, Mila chuckled under her breath. "I can't come down for dinner tonight, sweetie. I'm in the middle of unpacking. I don't even have my bed put together. I've been sleeping on a mattress on the floor."

"Daddy could help you out. He's good at stuff like that."

This time her dad let out an audible sigh. "Shaylee—"

"You are. You put my bed together. You're big and strong and you're supposed to help out ladies like Mila when they need a hand. That's what Uncle Drew said when Amber moved in up here."

Liam muttered an oath and Mila continued to smile. It was apparent this guy had his hands full with this little bundle of energy. She was a kick in the pants.

"I can help you out if you want," he eventually offered after shooting his daughter a warning look.

Mila chuckled again. "Actually, I'm pretty strong and handy myself. But thanks anyway."

"Will you still come and meet Lucky?"

"Of course I will. Just let me get myself settled. Maybe in a day or two."

Shaylee looked disappointed. "Do you promise?"

"I promise," Mila assured her, falling a little in love. She just couldn't say no to the kid.

"Pinky swear?" Shaylee lifted up her pinky. "If you pinky swear, you can't break the promise. It's against the law."

Mila knelt down and offered her pinky finger.

"Well I am a police officer so I wouldn't think of breaking the law."

Shaylee's face broke into a smile and she gave Mila's pinky a shake.

"Okay, we've taken up enough of Ms. Barnes' time," Liam intervened. "Go downstairs and wash your hands for dinner. Use soap and make sure you rinse good. I'll be there in a minute."

Shaylee turned and scampered down the stairs.

Liam's eyes lifted and connected with Mila's. "Sorry about that. We're working on the whole stranger danger thing. She's a little too friendly for her own good."

"She's very charming," Mila replied honestly.

"She is. She won't be a pest so don't worry. She's used to running up here all the time. Amber was her teacher at school, as well as Drew's girl, so they're pretty tight."

"I figured as much."

They stood there silently for another minute.

Eventually, he straightened. "I should get back downstairs." He hesitated, then shrugged. "I really can help you out if you need it. She's right, I should have offered myself. I worked an all-nighter last night and picked her up this morning so I'm a little out of sorts. Lack of sleep."

"I've got it covered. And don't be too hard on

her. She didn't bother me at all. I don't know a lot of people around here so it's nice to know my neighbors."

He considered her. "Sleeping during the day and working at night, you probably won't see the best Portland has to offer."

"Probably not. Occupational hazard."

"I hear you." He gave her a salute. "I'm sure I'll see you around."

"I'm sure." She watched as he disappeared down the stairs. When he was out of sight, she stepped back into her apartment. For some reason there was a smile on her face. When she realized it was there, she rolled her eyes. What the hell was she grinning about?

She gave Liam Colson another thought. There was no denying he was attractive. Good looking in a classic kind of way. The tall, dark and handsome thing. Rugged and engaging.

Pushing the notion aside, she turned back to the moving boxes that threatened to swallow her up and got to work.

2

Liam cleared the dishes from the table and set them in the sink, prepared to rinse them for the dishwasher. Before he could get started, there was a knock on the door.

His mind immediately shot straight to thoughts of his new neighbor. Had she run into trouble and needed his help after all?

"Can I answer it?" Shaylee asked, making a beeline for the door.

He snagged her at the last minute and lifted her into his arms. "I told you to go into your room and get your pajamas ready. If you want your thirty minutes of story time, you'd better get to it." He set her down and gave her a gentle shove in the direction of her room.

Frowning, she did as she was told.

Shaking his head, he opened the door. He didn't find Mila Barnes on the doorstep. Instead, he found Drew standing there, a paper bag in his hand.

"Ice cream. I promised the kid." Drew stepped inside without an invitation and held the bag up. "She's not in bed is she?"

"No." Liam kicked the door shut. "But I'm not sure she needs ice cream so late at night. She had cookies after dinner."

"You're only a kid once. Where is she?" Drew set the ice cream down on the counter and helped himself to a couple of bowls from the cabinet next to the refrigerator. "You want some? Chocolate with peanut butter. Who can turn that down?"

"I'm good." Liam went to work loading the dishwasher. "I really wish you and Amber would pop out a kid of your own so you'll quit spoiling the hell out of mine."

"Even if I did have a kid of my own, I'd still spoil yours. Why are you so crabby?" Drew set the remainder of the ice cream in the freezer.

"I'm not crabby."

"You are. Ice cream will help. Trust me."

"No, thanks. Where's Amber?"

"Her friend's in town. Reagan. Remember her?"

He vaguely remembered hearing about

Amber's friend from Seattle. "She's married to the cop, right?"

"They're not married. They got engaged a few months ago."

Liam leaned back against the counter. "Interesting. I've got a bone to pick with you."

"With me?" Drew eyed his brother curiously. "What did I do?"

"My daughter is barely six years old, Drew. I don't think she needs to know why you frequently visited Amber upstairs when she first moved in."

Drew frowned, apparently still confused.

Liam arched a brow. "It's only right for big, strong men like ourselves to offer our services to a lady when she's in need of assistance."

Drew's lips broke into a smile. "Oh, that. Well, I had to tell her something when I kept popping up to Amber's. Would you rather I told her the truth?"

"Absolutely not." Liam grimaced. "She took off upstairs today and accosted my new neighbor."

"Mila?" Drew shrugged. "So, what? She's cool."

"For one thing, I didn't know where she was. I looked like an idiot when I went up there shouting after her."

"Dude, it's right upstairs. And you know

Mila's a cop. Slade and I told you all about her."

"That's not the point. Shaylee put me on the spot and invited the woman down here for dinner. It was awkward as hell."

Drew outright laughed. "That kid is something else."

"I really don't think this is funny."

Drew continued to smile. "Who do you think set Amber and I up?"

It was true. Shaylee had pulled off a similar shenanigan on Amber and Drew when they'd first met. Still, he didn't see the humor in things at the moment. "I had a talk with her at dinner. She's not supposed to be openly gabbing with strangers and she's sure as hell not supposed to be inviting them over to dinner."

"Mila's not really a total stranger," Drew argued, swallowing some ice cream. "I mean both Slade and I have talked about her in front of Shaylee. Sammy probably has, too. I doubt if Shaylee considered her dangerous."

Liam was still annoyed, although he figured his brother was partly right.

Lucky chose that moment to let out a yowl from somewhere in the back of the apartment. Liam grimaced, figuring the cat was probably on his bed. The damned thing had taken permanent residency there. With Shaylee gone every other week, the irritating feline didn't like sleeping alone. The problem was, Liam did. He was having a hell of a time training the animal to obey his commands. "That's another thing," he griped, gesturing to the hallway. "That freaking cat. What the hell were you thinking with that?"

Drew shrugged innocently. "Shaylee wanted a pet. You said no dog in the apartment because you're gone so much. Cats are loners. They like being by themselves."

"Lucky is no loner. He sleeps on my neck and snores in my ear all night long. When I try to move him, he hisses at me. He's scratching the crap out of my stuff and he's stinking up the place with his litter box. I'm going to let Shaylee take him to Shelby's next week when she leaves."

"Shelby's allergic to cats. That's why I thought Shaylee should have the cat here."

"*Pam's* allergic to cats, not Shelby," Liam corrected, and bristled again. The last thing he wanted to do was think about his ex and her current significant other. The fact that his wife had left him for a woman still rankled. He'd been clueless and caught completely by surprise when she'd outed herself from the closet and filed for divorce. It had been months and the relationship he had with Shelby and Pam was still strained at best. The two women were now living together and engaged.

If he were being honest, he had to admit that Pam was good to Shaylee. His daughter liked her well enough—even looked forward to seeing her. She was good with kids and always willing to pick up the slack when Shelby or Liam had conflicting schedules. Still…

"You're going to have to get over this crap, Liam. Move on. It's been months."

"I don't need you to remind me of that."

"Don't you? You haven't even been on a date."

"I've been on a date. Three actually." He frowned thoughtfully. All three dates had been lousy. And it hadn't been the fault of the women he'd taken out. He knew that. He was like a fish out of water these days. He just didn't know how to get back in the saddle, so to speak.

"You were an ace at this crap before you met Shelby," Drew pointed out.

Appreciating his brother's encouragement, he let out a sigh. "I'm thirty-one years old now, Drew. And I've got a six-year-old to think about. It's not about me anymore."

"Not entirely. But some of it has to be. If you're miserable, it will eventually rub off on Shaylee."

Liam knew that was true.

"Listen, I know you've been through a lot. I don't condone what Shelby did. It downright sucked. But Pam does care about Shaylee and Shaylee cares about her. You could do worse for a prospective stepparent for your daughter."

Liam was just childish enough to be annoyed at the comment. "You just know it all, don't you?"

"I'm pretty damn smart," Drew chortled. "Middle children are always smarter."

"You're making that up. And you're only a few minutes behind me. I very well could have been second."

"But you weren't."

Drew had been ten minutes behind Liam. Slade had come along five minutes after that.

"This is a stupid conversation," Liam snapped, just as another knock sounded on the door. He grimaced and walked over to answer it. This time it was Mila Barnes standing on the doorstep.

Automatically, he found himself giving her another look. He'd noticed she was attractive earlier. She stood a little over five feet tall. She had reddish-brown hair that reached just below her shoulders and was currently held back by a bandana she wore around her head. The jeans she had on were form-fitting and dusty. So was the black T-shirt she wore.

"I'm sorry to bother you. I hope you weren't sleeping."

"I wasn't," he said automatically. "I'm just getting Shaylee settled for bed. What's up?"

"If you meant what you said earlier, I could use a hand." She folded her arms over her chest uncomfortably. "I got the bed frame together but lifting the box spring and mattress by myself is a bit more of a chore than I expected."

"Go," Drew said, appearing behind Liam suddenly. "I'll get the kid ready for bed and read her a story." He grinned over Liam's shoulder at Mila. "Hey, Mila. How's it going?"

"Hi, Drew. I didn't know you were here."

"Brought the kid some ice cream." He gave Liam a shove. "Go help her out. I've got this."

Liam bit back a scowl.

An awkward silence ensued and he felt Drew's elbow in his ribs. He fought back the urge to punch his brother. Quickly gathering his composure, he stepped into the hallway, promptly shutting the door in Drew's face.

Mila was already on the stairs. "I really am sorry to bother you. I know you said you worked all night. It won't take long to toss the bed together."

"It's not a big deal." He followed her up to the apartment. He'd been inside before. When Amber had lived there it had been decorated with trendy artwork and stylish furniture. It had been spotless each and every time he'd been there.   Right now, the place was in a bit of a disarray, most likely because Mila had just moved in.

"Excuse the mess. I'll get it unpacked sooner or later." She led him into the bedroom where a simple, metal frame was set up in the middle of the floor.

"If you can grab one end, I'll grab the other." She gestured to the queen-sized box spring nearby.

"You want me to double check the bolts in the frame?"

She arched a brow. "Like you don't think I got them tight enough myself?"

He arched one back. "I didn't say that. I just figured another set of hands isn't a bad idea."

She backed up and gestured to the bed frame. "Have at it."

He'd hit a nerve. He could see that clearly. "It's your bed."

"Please. I'll feel better if you check."

There was something in her eyes that told him that wasn't the case at all. Still, figuring there was no way around it, he crouched and went at the bolts with an Allen wrench. To his surprise, they were all tightened perfectly.

When he straightened, he noticed the smug smile on her face. For a little thing, she apparently had hulk strength.

He tossed the wrench aside and they went to work moving the box spring and mattress into their proper positions on the frame.

When that was done, he helped her push the bed back against the wall near the room's one window.

"Thank you." She'd lost the smirk and was just smiling now.

"You're welcome."

She led him back to the living room. When they reached the front door, he turned and met her gaze. "Can I ask you something?"

"I have an older brother. He taught me everything from Karate to bow hunting. I may be small but I know how to take care of myself." She didn't even blink. "Not only that, I was in the army. I know how to do man's work. Does that answer your question?"

He found himself more impressed than he wanted to be. He folded his arms over his chest, his lips quirking. "You were in the army?"

"I was. I did four years of active duty. I finished out my enlistment in the reserves and went to school. Then I became a cop."

"I was Navy."

"And now you work for the fire department. I'm surprised you're not a cop, too."

"I thought about it. I've always taken a liking to the medical side of things. Planned on going to medical school but..." His voice trailed off and he kept the explanation of why he never made it to med school to himself. He wasn't about to spill details of his marital nightmare to her.

"Life got in the way," she figured out for herself.

"Something like that," he agreed. "I came home and applied with the fire department and the rest is history."

"My days as a soldier weren't the happiest I've experienced but they formed me into the person I am today. I'm grateful for the discipline. I wouldn't be doing what I'm doing now if it wasn't for my time in the military."

"Agreed." He was somewhat intrigued by the fact that they shared a similar philosophy. Of course, he'd shared that same philosophy with Shelby and look where that had gotten him. He turned toward the door.

"You think you could do one more thing for me before you go?"

He met her gaze again. "Sure."

"I'm strong but I can't grow ten inches, and you are a firefighter. I've got a smoke detector that I can't reach, even on a chair. I'm going to pick up a ladder tomorrow but in the meantime, it's chirping. Do you mind?"

He followed her gaze to a corner of the dining

room, where as if on cue, a smoke detector let out a shrill beep. "You got a battery?"

She dug through a box nearby and offered him a rectangular battery.

The chore took him seconds to complete. He tested the detector to be sure it was working before he climbed down from the chair. "Any others?"

"Nope. No other beeping."

"I can change them anyway if you want me to. When one goes, they all eventually follow."

She considered that, then offered him the package that held the remainder of the batteries.

It didn't take him long to replace the others.

When he was through, she glanced at her watch. "I'm sorry. It's after eight. I didn't mean to keep you this long."

"It's not a big deal. It's my civic duty." He grinned halfway.

She smiled back. "I guess technically it is when you're on the clock. I owe you."

"You don't. After Shaylee put you on the spot earlier…" He shrugged. "Let's just call it even."

"She didn't put me on the spot. She was just being friendly. I don't mind meeting her cat."

"You might when you meet him. He's an asshole."

She started to laugh. "Not a cat person, huh?"

"Not in the least."

"So why did you give in?"

"I didn't. My brother did. Shaylee wanted a puppy. I said no while we're living in the apartment and we're both gone so much. She spends every other week with her mom. Drew thought a cat would be better." He rolled his eyes and she laughed again.

"I should go." He opened the door and stepped into the hallway. At the last minute, he turned. "Earlier, I was going to ask you something. We kind of got off the beaten path when you brought up the military."

She waited for him to say more.

"When you saw Drew behind me tonight, you knew immediately who he was. I've got family that can't tell us apart. How did you know he wasn't Slade?"

She thought about that for a moment. "I don't know. I just did. I worked with both of them at the same time and I guess I can hear differences in their voices. One has hair longer than the other. You're all different if a person takes the time to figure that out."

Impressed, he eyed her curiously. Then he threw caution to the wind, without giving it much thought. "If you're hurting for a meal this week, you really are welcome to come downstairs and knock on the door. I cook most nights when Shay's with me. There's plenty."

"You don't need to feel obligated."

"I don't. I should have offered myself. Like I said earlier, I'm out of sorts. A few hours of sleep and I'll be good as new."

She leaned against the doorjamb. "I appreciate the offer. Maybe I'll take you up on it sometime."

He took the stairs two at a time and headed back to his apartment. Drew was sitting on the couch thumbing through a magazine when he walked inside. Arching a brow, his brother gave him a look. "Took you long enough. You try the mattress out or something?"

"Don't be a dick. Where's Shaylee?"

"I read her a story and she fell asleep halfway through. Lucky's in there with her. You can thank me later."

"I'll thank you now."

Drew stood and grabbed his keys from the coffee table. "She's cute, man."

Liam faced his brother, knowing he wasn't talking about Shaylee. "Butt out."

"I am butting out. I'm just giving you my two cents."

"How is that butting out?"

"Butting in is what Shaylee did." Drew grinned. "I'm just saying…"

"Go home," Liam warned. "I'm going to bed."

"Okay, okay. I'll talk to you tomorrow." Drew left and Liam headed for his bedroom. He quickly changed into a pair of boxer briefs and climbed into his bed. Just as he was about to fall asleep, he felt the mattress give a little. The next thing he knew, the freaking cat was nestled snuggly next to his head, snoring away.

He made a mental note to throttle Drew the next time he saw him.

3

When Mila walked into Precinct 124 on Sunday evening just before midnight, the place was pretty empty. There was nobody on the desk so she walked back through a maze of cubicles until she found a room with lockers in it. Her name was taped to one near the front and she tossed her things into it and checked her appearance in the mirror nearby.

On patrol, the uniform required was dark blue. The cargo pants were warm and thick, the shirt with her name on it, matching. She made sure her radio was correctly connected and double checked her weapon before sliding her jacket on.

"You Barnes?"

Hearing the male voice, she turned. She found a tall man with thinning blond hair and blue eyes staring down at her. He looked around the same age as her twenty-seven years. His name patch read *Ledbetter*.

Her partner. She knew she was paired up with an officer named Bryan Ledbetter.

She smiled easily. "That's right. I'm Barnes. I guess you and I are partners."

"It seems that way. At least for now. You ready?"

She didn't miss the hint of resentment in his voice. How did he already have a negative opinion of her when he didn't even know her?

"Just so you know, I run my shift nice and tidy. I like to be on the beat at exactly midnight. I'm out at eight AM," he informed her, motioning with his finger for her to follow him.

Having no choice, she trailed in his wake.

"I'm by the book," he continued. "I don't screw around. I hold my own. I expect you to do the same." They exited through a door in the rear of the precinct and out into the crisp, September air. He pushed a button on the key fob he held and a chirping sound came from a patrol car parked nearby. "I drive. I don't make a good passenger. Is that a problem?"

She wanted to say yes. With Winters, he'd always insisted on driving. Once he'd been promoted, she'd taken control of her own patrol car. Now she was back to being in the passenger seat again.

He cleared his throat and she realized he was staring at her over the roof of the vehicle, waiting for her to answer the question.

Meeting his gaze head on, she shrugged. "Whatever works best."

"I don't want any mistakes here, Barnes. I don't know what your story is where you came from, but I'm assuming there's a reason you're here. Don't bring baggage with you. I'm on the fast track to bigger and better things. Don't screw that up for me."

"With all due respect, I haven't even gotten in the car with you yet."

"I know how you women work. Personally, I'm not a fan of females on the force. I figure it's fair that I warn you I don't plan to pick up any slack for you. Keep your tears to yourself and your nose to the grindstone. You get me?"

Immediately irritated, she frowned at him. Before she could say anything, their radio crackled. They had a call that needed attention.

"Let's go." He slid into the driver's seat and flipped on the siren. Accepting that she'd most likely just gone from one bad situation to a worse one, she bit the bullet and slid into the vehicle.

Her first shift did not go well. She felt stiff as

a board sitting in the vehicle next to Ledbetter. He didn't warm up to her as the hours went by. In fact, he seemed even frostier by the time they headed back to the station to drop off their vehicle, just before eight the next morning.

Still, she gave herself a peptalk. She was the new kid on the block, so to speak. She was going to have to prove herself to her new colleagues.

As the week wore on, she grew more weary and far more skeptical. Ledbetter was a tough nut to crack. He didn't make any more inappropriate comments about her gender but he did make sure she held her own on the job.

During a very stressful traffic stop involving a drunk man who was probably three times her size, Ledbetter leaned against their patrol car and left her completely on her own to handle the unstable situation.

When the man took a swing at her, she had no choice but subdue him herself, which wasn't easy. By the time she had him cuffed and in the back of the cruiser, she was out of breath and angry as hell. She slammed the door to the vehicle and rounded on Ledbetter. "I could have used some help there."

He lifted his head from the handheld computer he was typing in and eyed her with a smirk on his face. Catching onto her anger, he snorted. "Seems to me, you handled it fine yourself. You didn't ask me for any assistance. I wouldn't want to overstep. That's a touchy thing in this day and age."

It was on the tip of her tongue to point out that he'd already labeled her the weaker sex. Instead, she bit the retort back and walked away from him.

A couple of days later, they were in a similar situation with a strung-out, female drug addict who was caught attempting to break into a Rite Aid. Again, Ledbetter stood aside with the handheld and took notes while she did all the dirty work herself.

By the time Friday came around, she was exhausted, frustrated and genuinely pissed off. This guy was worse than Jeff Winters. The idea was almost unfathomable.

"Coffee stop," he said, interrupting her misery as he pulled the patrol car to the side of the road in front of a trendy café. It was a little after six in the morning and the place had just opened. "You want anything?"

"No, thanks," she said quietly, determined to keep her temper in check.

"I'll be back." He left the vehicle and disappeared inside the restaurant. He was gone for at least twenty minutes before she peered through the window to see what had happened to him. He was just visible at the front counter.

Irritated, she watched as he laughed with the barista on duty and appeared not to have a care in the world.

When a patrol car pulled up and parked nearby, she stiffened. She recognized Carter Brubaker, another officer with the PPB, as he stepped to the pavement and glanced her way. Finley Jones, his current partner, followed suit.

Sighing as they headed her way, Mila reluctantly rolled down the window and planted a firm smile in place. This poker face thing was getting harder and harder as time went on.

"How's it going?" Brubaker greeted, stepping up to her side of the vehicle and giving her an easy smile.

Carter Brubaker was a couple of years younger than she was. She'd met him earlier in the week. He was blond and blue-eyed. Around six feet tall, he had a decent build. He was one of the friendlier officers she'd met so far. Naturally, she hadn't gotten lucky enough to be paired with him.

"It's good," she forced out. "You?"

"Just grabbing some java." He indicated the officer behind him. "Have you met Finley Jones? She's been on the desk for the past few months. She's new to the beat."

Mila smiled in Finley's direction. The woman was a knockout with brown hair and round, expressive eyes. "I don't think we've met officially. I live upstairs from Shaylee Colson. She speaks highly of you."

Finley chuckled, shaking her head. "That kid… She's a doll. She'll keep you on your toes."

"I've figured that out already," Mila agreed.

"You're with Ledbetter, right?" Carter questioned.

She grimaced involuntarily and nodded.

Carter surprised her by snorting. "He's a dick. I was stuck with him for a while. You need to stand your ground and he'll back off. He's got some connections in the department. He's a blue blood. His grandfather was a step away from chief when he retired. Two of his uncles were notorious, too, one with the bomb squad, one with Vice. He likes to think he's important."

"Which he's not," Finley added, rolling her eyes. She gave Mila a sympathetic smile. "I feel for you. You got stuck with him because nobody else can work with him. We're short-staffed right now so there's no firing him just for being a—"

"Ms. Jones. Nice to see you." Ledbetter was suddenly there at the car. He gave Finley a saccharine smile.

Finley ignored him and gestured to her partner. "We should go. It was nice to meet you." She tossed a wave toward Mila.

"Yeah, you, too." Mila rolled up her window, a bad taste in her mouth.

"What did you say to them?" Ledbetter demanded as he slid into the driver's seat. He offered her a coffee. "Here. I was trying to bring you a peace offering. Obviously it was a moot gesture."

"I didn't say anything to them. They came up to me and Brubaker introduced me to Jones." She begrudgingly accepted the coffee, more to keep the peace than for any other reason.

Ledbetter started up the car. "You know complaining will only keep you in the shitter. It would serve you well to realize that."

She clenched her teeth and kept silent. He was goading her and she knew better than to fall into his trap.

The radio crackled at that moment. There was a domestic dispute call that needed their attention. Without comment, Ledbetter responded to dispatch, lit the vehicle up and they headed for the scene. When they got there, they found fire and paramedics were already there.

She and Ledbetter went to the door and he thumped his knuckles against the screen. They both backed up and waited.

According to dispatch, the homeowners were a thirty-something couple named Kendall. The husband had a history of domestic abuse. There had been multiple calls from the neighbors surrounding them in the past.

It took several seconds for someone to answer. A tall man with a long beard eventually whipped open the door angrily. "What the hell do you want?"

After they identified themselves, Ledbetter did his usual and stepped back, allowing her to take the floor.

Sensing she was in over her head again, she gave herself another silent peptalk. She'd handled the other two maniacs. She could handle this creep. "Mr. Kendall, we need to speak to your wife."

"She's busy." He attempted to shut the door in her face.

"Before I can leave, I'll need to speak with her," Mila insisted. "We received a call from one of your neighbors, reporting a disturbance. We're going to need to be sure your wife is okay."

"She's fine," the man said angrily. "That fucking busybody next door doesn't know what she's talking about. I know it was her that called. She's always butting into our business."

Mila glanced over her shoulder at Ledbetter. He merely shrugged his shoulders.

Clenching her teeth again, she turned back to

Mr. Kendall. "I'm going to need to speak with your wife. Once we know she's okay, we'll be on our way."

"Like I said," Kendall seethed, reaching for the screen door and whipping it open so abruptly he nearly tagged Mila in the face. "My wife is fine. You're going to have to take my word for that."

Refusing to let him bully her, she stood her ground. "I don't think so. If you refuse to cooperate I'm going to have to take you down to the station." She nodded over her shoulder at Ledbetter to call for back up.

"I don't think so, sweetheart." Kendall reached for her face, his fingers biting into the flesh of her jaw hard enough to make her wince. She reacted on instinct. She used a military move and despite the fact that he outweighed her by at least a hundred pounds, she was able to drop him to his knees. Unfortunately, he didn't stay there. He was up and coming at her again before she could react.

Ledbetter stepped forward in time to be knocked sideways and into the nearby shrubbery.

After that, things escalated very quickly. Mila went for her weapon just as Liam Colson stepped in front of her from out of nowhere and with a very impressive military move of his own, took Mr. Kendall down in one swift swoop. He jammed a booted foot into the man's back and spoke very firmly as the guy struggled. "Stay down."

Mila had her cuffs out immediately and while Liam held the flailing jerk down, she managed to manacle his wrists.

Two patrol cars screeched to a halt in front of the residence and Carter Brubaker and Finley Jones joined Mila on the porch seconds later.

Ignoring the pain in her jaw, Mila helped them drag a still very unruly Mr. Kendall to his feet. The man was hauled from the scene and stowed in the back of a patrol car.

"What the hell were you doing?" Ledbetter suddenly appeared, his expression full of fury.

Mila worked her jaw back and forth and the pain there grew more intense. "Excuse me?" she managed to mutter.

"He could have killed me!" Ledbetter raged, pulling several brambles from his thinning hair. "What the hell were you thinking, not calling for backup? That guy was three times your size!"

"I asked *you* to call for backup," she argued, glaring at him. A headache was beginning to burn behind her eyes and she felt a little sick to her stomach.

"Was that what you were doing? I can't read your fucking lips, Barnes." Ledbetter shook his head in disgust. "Your jaw is turning purple. Go get it looked at."

It was on the tip of Mila's tongue to tell the guy to go to hell. She shut her eyes and counted to ten inside her head. When she opened again, he was still standing there glowering at her. "I'm fine. I don't need to be looked at."

"Department policy. Go. I'll handle this from here." He already had his phone in his hand.

Defeated, she turned toward the ambulance. As if she weren't mortified enough, Liam Colson was standing at the bottom of the steps watching the entire exchange. He was frowning in Ledbetter's direction. "He's right. You should get that jaw looked at." He spoke to her but he was still glaring at Ledbetter.

"It's just bruised. I'm fine." She stalked past him and toward a waiting ambulance. She could see a woman was already seated inside. She stopped, watching as the paramedics—Jacy Colson, a recent hire to the fire department, being one of them—worked on the injured female.

She realized suddenly that this was probably Mrs. Kendall. The woman was a mess. Her makeup was smeared with tears and her hands were shaking violently. There were bruises and contusions marring both her upper arms.

Mila stopped short and listened while Jacy

did her best to provide first aid. Mrs. Kendall wasn't making things easy. She was more concerned with the fact that her husband was hunkered over in the back of a police car.

"Where are you taking him?"

It took Mila a few seconds to figure out the woman was speaking to her. She answered curtly. "To jail."

"No! He didn't do anything! This is all a big misunderstanding!"

Jacy and Mila exchanged glances. Mila took the floor. "You will have your opportunity to explain things down at the station. If you choose not to press charges, that's your prerogative. He will, however, be facing charges for assaulting an officer. Two officers, actually. You might want to get him a lawyer."

"A lawyer!" Mrs. Kendall started to sob. "We can't afford a lawyer!"

Mila could see this woman was a textbook version of an abused spouse. This wasn't her first rodeo. There would be no convincing her to do the right thing.

"You should have that jaw looked at," Jacy said, stepping down from the ambulance. She let another paramedic, a woman Mila didn't know, take over with Mrs. Kendall.

"It's not broken. I'd know if it was." Mila let Jacy give her a quick onceover for paperwork purposes.

"It's going to be black and blue tomorrow. They can probably give you something for the pain if you go into Emergency."

"I don't do pain pills." Mila watched as Mrs. Kendall fought her way from the back of the ambulance and took off across the yard toward the patrol car where her husband was still confined.

"Some people just don't want help," Jacy remarked, shaking her head. She tucked a long strand of dark hair behind her ear and gathered her things together. "Are you sure you don't want a ride in? The bureau has rules about stuff like this."

"I'm fine. You looked me over." She stepped away and allowed Jacy and her co-worker to pack up their things.

She rode back to the precinct with Ledbetter even though she didn't want to.

"Listen," he said when they were a block or so from their destination. "I'm willing to chalk this one up to a bit of miscommunication if you are. I mean we're new partners. We're still figuring this thing with us out. No harm, no foul."

She found her teeth clenching again.

"Did you hear me?"

"I heard you, Ledbetter." She spoke quietly.

"Okay. So we've got each other's backs?"

Was he serious?

She cast a sidelong glance his way.

He was, she realized. Stiffening, she glared at him. "You've put me in this position all week long, just to prove a point. Don't turn this around on me."

"That's not what I was doing," he said, stammering a little. Then his eyes darkened. "Look, I'm trying to be reasonable here. Let's just start over. It's the best solution for both of us."

A voice in her head told her that he was liable to get her killed if she let him bully her into silence. Another voice told her she was going to be blacklisted if she complained. She was a newbie to this department. And Ledbetter wasn't.

They pulled into the parking lot, still silent. She refused to give him the satisfaction of knowing he was rattling her.

She went straight to her locker without speaking to anyone and changed her clothes. Thankfully the room was empty. Most people had already started or left their shifts.

Using the bathroom tap, she splashed some cold water on her face and glanced into the mirror above the sink. There was a purpling bruise forming just below her right cheek. It was going to be hell to cover.

Sighing, she cursed Ledbetter yet again. *The bastard.* As impossible as it seemed, she'd run across the one man who was worse than Jeff Winters.

Grabbing her things, she made her way out of the locker room. She was hoping to exit the building without any unnecessary altercations.

No such luck.

Just as she reached the main lobby, Captain Ray Tennant stepped in front of her, a concerned expression on his face.

In the last week since she'd started with the PPB, she'd interacted with Tennant more than once. He was a hands-on kind of captain. He kept a very tight rein on his people. He was in his late fifties. His once dark hair had long since turned gray and he carried a few extra pounds around his waist. He was a tall man—an intimidating man.

In other words, he wasn't someone whose bad side she wanted to get on, especially during her first week on the job.

"Barnes. I'd like to speak to you in my office before you head out."

She knew right away it wasn't a request.

Tail between her legs, she followed him down the hallway, ignoring the looks tossed her way from the other officers in the room.

"Shut the door," Tennant ordered, taking a

seat behind his large, somewhat messy desk.

Mila did as she was told.

"Sit. Just toss those papers over here," he instructed, gesturing to a stack of file folders that were covering the chair in front of his desk.

She hated to add to the administrative chaos and hesitated.

"It's not as disorganized as it looks." He held out his hands for the files.

She scooped them up and gave them to him, then sat down.

"How's the jaw?"

"It's fine, sir."

"It doesn't look fine. It looks purple. You have it checked out?"

"I did." She was thankful now, that she'd allowed Jacy to take a look at her injury. Something told her Tennant would have had her head if she hadn't.

"What happened?"

She figured Ledbetter had already given his side of the story. She thought about how to answer the question carefully. Her career was on the line here.

"Ledbetter filled out a report," he continued. "I'm sure he was thorough but I'd like to hear from you, as well. Incidents like this—when things go awry—don't go unnoticed."

Her back stiff, she tried to settle her nerves

down. It was no use. Tennant was staring her straight in the eyes and it was making her anxiety worse.

He leaned back, steepling his fingers in front of him. "I realize you're only a few days into this gig. There's an adjustment period. If you made a mistake, just say so. Your job isn't on the line. Not at this point."

It was on the tip of her tongue to toss Ledbetter to the wolves. The problem was, she wasn't sure if those wolves would listen to her. Ledbetter was one of them.

"Barnes, you come highly recommended." Tennant relaxed a little and dropped his hands to his desk blotter. "Detective Haynes is one of my best guys. He's got good instincts and he saw something special in you. That's why you're here. That being said, you need to be able to act as a team player. We have to have each other's backs out there. If we don't, people die. You understand what I'm trying to tell you?"

"Yes, sir." She didn't break eye contact, knowing Tennant wouldn't respect her one bit if she did.

He stared at her for a long time. "Are you sure there's nothing you want to add to Ledbetter's report?"

"I didn't see the report, sir." She honestly had no idea how Ledbetter had managed to submit a report so quickly. They'd only been back at the station for thirty minutes or so.

Tennant slid a piece of paper toward her and waited while she skimmed the gist of it.

Surprisingly, Ledbetter wasn't entirely throwing her under the bus. He was claiming the attack was so sudden neither of them had a chance to call for back up at first.

She slid the report back across the desk silently.

"Nothing you want to add?" Tennant prodded, still looking her in the eye.

She swallowed her pride and shook her head. "I think he covered everything."

"Okay then. Go home and ice that jaw up. It will help with the swelling. If it gets any worse and you need further medical attention, don't hesitate. Just be sure you fill out the proper paperwork for an on-the-job injury. Take a couple of days off and we'll see you back Monday."

Sensing her dismissal, she got up and left the office. Even once she was behind the wheel of her car, she didn't relax. She gripped the steering wheel tightly and rested her head against it, breathing deeply.

Her phone began to ring and she glanced at the irritating device. Reid was calling.

Knowing better than to answer her brother's

call in the shape she was in, she ignored him and started up her vehicle. At this point, she wanted nothing more than to soak in a hot bath and go to bed.

4

Liam got home just after eight that morning. He'd survived a long, long shift. Multiple calls. All complicated. He was exhausted. Shaylee was back at her mother's for the week so he had nothing to stop him from getting a few hours of sleep.

Only he couldn't sleep. The minute his head hit the pillow, he found himself staring up at the ceiling instead of falling into the dreamless sleep he desired.

Lucky slithered up the comforter and sat near his head. Immediately, the cat began to lick its paws.

Rolling his eyes, Liam glared in the feline's direction. He supposed he could toss the cat out in the living room and shut the door but the last time he'd done so, the damn cat had meowed for a good hour before finally worming his way back into the room.

Again, he wanted to throttle his brother.

Eventually, Lucky settled down.

Still, Liam couldn't sleep. His body was fatigued but his mind was wide awake. And he knew exactly why.

Turning over, he slapped at his pillow and dropped his head into the middle of it. He told himself to forget about the last call he'd gone on that morning. He told himself to forget about *her*.

But he couldn't.

The situation had been a shit show from the beginning. When the fire department had arrived on scene, Michael Kendall had been belligerent, refusing to open the door—refusing to allow his wife medical attention. Theoretically, the arrival of the police should have diffused things.

Instead, quite the opposite had occurred.

He had to admit, catching Mila Barnes in action was a sight to see. She'd taken Michael Kendall—a two-hundred-some-odd-pound, angry man to his knees, with very little effort. Unfortunately the move hadn't been enough to keep the creep there. At the time, Liam had sensed things taking a very ugly turn. And they had. In fact, everything spun out of control so quickly, he'd barely made it there in time to help Mila. Another minute and Kendall would have had his meaty fingers wrapped around her throat.

He swore, turning over again. He wasn't the chauvinistic type. He was a firm believer that women were smart, capable human beings. He worked with a couple of women at the firehouse that gave him a run for his money where strength testing was concerned. But the fact of the matter was, size did matter. And Mila Barnes had been out-sized that morning. All the military training in the world couldn't change that fact.

Liam's jaw tightened as he thought about the way her partner had stood back in the shadows and let her fend for herself. He didn't know the guy. Not personally. They'd crossed paths once or twice on the job but they'd never so much as exchanged a hello. So what was the guy's deal?

No answer came to mind. Swearing, he turned again, eliciting a hiss from the cat as he rolled on the little bastard's long tail. "Move," he snapped, giving the cat a gentle shove.

He received another hiss for his efforts.

Flopping onto his back, he gave up and let the cat burrow into his neck.

For the next three hours, he tossed and turned. Eventually, just after noon, he gave up and slid from his bed.

After a long, hot shower and a fresh change of clothes, he felt a bit more human. He brewed a pot of coffee and glanced at the morning paper. Bad news. Nothing unusual.

Strolling over to the front door, he peered out into the street. His truck was there, parked where he always parked it, right at the curb. In front of it, he saw the red SUV. He knew it belonged to Mila. He'd seen her pull up in it a couple of times over the past week.

She hadn't been home when he'd gotten there earlier. He supposed there was probably follow-up after an incident like the one she'd gone through that morning.

He sipped his coffee and tried to talk himself out of being concerned about her. She'd assured him she was fine. She'd assured his sister she was fine — refused medical attention.

Still, he'd seen the purple bruise forming on her jaw. And he'd seen the stressed look in her eyes.

Deciding that checking on her was the neighborly thing to do, he set his coffee aside and made his way up the stairs to her apartment. Once he was there, he started to second-guess himself. She was probably sleeping. And even if she wasn't, she was surely in a terrible mood.

He hesitated, then figured the hell with it and rapped on the door.

A few seconds went by before he heard rustling on the other side. Eventually, it opened.

He took a minute and looked her over critically before he spoke. Unfortunately, she looked like hell. She was dressed in red flannel pajamas with poodles all over them. Her hair was up in a haphazard ponytail and her face was devoid of make-up. The bruise on her jaw was purple and prominent but the swelling had gone down.

"I'm sorry. I should have figured you'd be asleep." He leaned against the doorjamb. "I just thought I should check on you after…" His words trailed off and he shrugged. "After what happened this morning."

She scratched her chin sleepily, then winced, obviously forgetting about the bruise. "Go ahead and come in. Welcome to my nightmare." She stepped away from the door and padded into the kitchen without waiting for him.

He followed, shutting the door behind him. He noticed right away that the place was still chaotic with moving boxes. Apparently she hadn't been kidding about her expectations when it came to unpacking.

She was at the coffee pot by the time he

reached the kitchen. She had an empty bag of coffee grounds in her hands and was shaking the open bag upside down, a frustrated look on her face. She muttered a string of curses and tossed the bag aside. After a futile attempt at digging through a nearby box, she rubbed her hands over her face and groaned forlornly.

"I have some downstairs. I'm willing to share," he offered, a little amused at her state of disarray. He knew the feeling of despair one felt when realizing there was no coffee in the house.

"I already owe you for putting the batteries in my smoke detectors and helping me move my mattress." She bit her bottom lip skeptically. "I don't know how indebted to you I want to be."

He shrugged. "Suit yourself."

She only contemplated things for a moment before she grabbed a throw blanket from the couch and followed him toward the door. "Is your daughter home? I don't want her to see my face this way."

"She's with her mother this week. You don't have to worry about that."

Relieved, she trailed him down to his apartment where he poured her what was left in his coffee pot. Then he went to work brewing more.

"Thank you." She clasped the over-sized mug tightly between her fingers and took a long sip.

"There are some mornings when I honestly think I would kill for caffeine. This is one of those mornings."

He leaned back against the counter and crossed his ankles. "I know the feeling. I've run out a couple of times myself."

"I'm bad with grocery shopping. I put it off until the last minute. I can live on a box of crackers and block of cheese for a week."

He chuckled. "I might have done the same thing myself before I had a kid. The military humbles you."

"That's an understatement." She snuggled into her blanket and eyed him uneasily. "Do you mind if I take this upstairs? I know you probably have things to do today."

"Sit. I have no plans. You hungry?" He didn't wait for her to answer. He dug into the fridge and pulled out some eggs and bacon.

"You weren't kidding. You really cook that stuff?"

He arched a brow. "You can't cook an egg?"

She took another long sip of coffee then shrugged sheepishly. "At the risk of making myself more unappealing, no. I'm more of a processed food type of gal. My mother wasn't much of a cook either so I never really learned."

"What did you eat growing up then?" He tossed some eggs into a frying pan and added some cheese. Then he set the bacon to fry.

"Whatever was handy. Cereal. Crackers, cheese." She grinned. "I've got a real hankering for Cheez Whiz."

He snorted. "You and Shaylee are a match made in heaven." He indicated a seat near the breakfast bar when she continued to stand. "Sit down. This won't take long."

"I feel like I've bothered you a lot since I moved in." She didn't sit down.

"If you were bothering me, I'd let you know. Besides, *I* came up to see *you* today."

Her expression narrowed. "That's right. You did. Why?"

He stirred the eggs in the pan. "I was worried about you."

She didn't respond right away. The surprise in her eyes told him she wasn't used to such attention. That had him interested in her family life.

"I'm fine." She reluctantly sat down at the counter. "And I'd rather not talk about what happened this morning, if you don't mind."

He slid some eggs onto a plate and added a couple of pieces of bacon before sliding the food toward her. "Actually, I do mind." He stared at her for a long moment. "The whole situation was some bullshit."

She took a bite of bacon and chewed carefully.

"I've only been on the job here for a week. I'll learn the ropes soon."

He leaned back and braced himself against the counter. "I'm not certain it's you that needs to learn the ropes."

Again, she swallowed roughly. "I don't know what you're talking about."

"Your partner damn near let you get killed."

She gave her coffee her full attention again.

"Why do I get the feeling there's more going on here than meets the eye?" he prodded.

"There's nothing going on. You're blowing this whole thing out of proportion."

He leaned over so their eyes met. "I realize you're a woman doing a job that's primarily done by men. I'm sure that it's not always easy being taken seriously. That being said, Michael Kendall outweighs you by at least a hundred pounds. Do you really think it was smart for Ledbetter to stand back in the shadows and let you fend for yourself?"

"I did okay."

He snorted. "Yeah, you did at first. You were able to take the asshole down. *Temporarily.* Ledbetter should have stepped in at that point and helped you out. He just stood there like an idiot. What's his problem?"

Sighing, she set her coffee cup down. "I didn't hit my mark. If I had—"

He didn't like what he was hearing at all and he interrupted her. "This isn't about you hitting your mark. It's about your partner not doing his job. If I hadn't stepped in—"

"I realize you were out of your element. I'm sorry it came to that."

He muttered an oath. "I wasn't out of my element. I could probably kill a man with my bare hands if I had to—even a man as big as Michael Kendall." He leveled her with a glare. "*You* were out of *your* element. And your partner did nothing to help you."

She blew out a breath and leaned back. "I suppose it looked that way."

"It didn't *look* that way. It *was* that way."

. . .

She shifted uncomfortably. It wasn't exactly a shock to her that Liam Colson had everything figured out. He was a first responder after all. He went to scenes like what had happened that morning all the time. He knew proper procedure.

"He's giving you a hard time, isn't he?"

She didn't confirm the hunch. She just drank her coffee in silence.

"Did you tell Tennant?"

Still, she remained silent.

"Mila?" he prodded, making no move to eat his own breakfast.

"No," she finally admitted.

He gaped at her incredulously. "Why not?"

"You don't know how this works, Liam. If you did, you wouldn't be asking me that question."

He let out a sigh. "Damn right I know how it works. I work with the fire department. It's a male dominated profession. You can damn well bet I won't allow any crap like that to go down in my firehouse."

"Says the man." She wanted the words back once they were out.

Shoving his food aside, he took a seat next to her. "It's against the law for him to treat you in a sexist way. You realize that, right?"

"Of course I do."

"Then why aren't you doing anything about it? You could have been killed this morning."

It was on the tip of her tongue to tell him about all the other times Ledbetter had left her hanging over the past week. Instead, she remained silent.

"If you don't want to talk to Tennant, talk to Sammy—or Drew. Hell, talk to Slade. They won't let something like this lie."

"They're detectives, not supervisors." She slid her empty coffee cup toward him with imploring eyes.

He reached for the pot and refilled her cup. "You're making excuses for the fact that you're allowing yourself to be treated this way."

Knowing he was right rankled and she stiffened. "I've been with the bureau for exactly one week. How do you think it will look if I already start filing complaints?"

He expelled a breath. "You can't keep working with the asshole."

"I can. I will. I don't quit."

"What about your last job? You walked away from that."

Irritated, she scowled. "That was different. You don't know anything about my situation in Eugene."

"I know it couldn't have been great or you wouldn't have left there."

Giving up on enjoying her coffee, she stood up. "Forget it. I'm too tired to run this race today. Thanks for the coffee." She turned to leave.

He stopped her with a hand on her arm. "You're right, I don't know anything about your situation in Eugene. Tell me about it."

"No. It's not relevant."

"Isn't it?"

"You hardly know me. Why do you even care?"

He was quiet for a long time. "I don't like to

see anyone treated unfairly. You're good at what you do. I saw that firsthand this morning. Not only that, Sammy mentioned what you did to help my sister. That's a cop with good instincts. You deserve better than what you're getting."

The admission got to her and she found herself facing him again. "I can handle Ledbetter. I've dealt with his type before. He's a very small man, after whatever power he can get."

He definitely wanted to argue with her. It wasn't hard to see that. Instead, he motioned to the breakfast bar. "Sit. I don't like to eat alone."

She contemplated him uncertainly. Part of her wanted to go back up to her apartment and climb under the covers where she could hide until she had to face the world again on Monday. Another part of her didn't want that at all. This guy intrigued her. Damn it, she liked him whether she wanted to or not.

"Admit it, I'm a pretty good cook."

He grinned and she couldn't help but smile back. He was trying to lighten the mood up. Thank God.

"You're okay. It's not the worst meal I've ever had."

"It's got to be a step up from Cheez Whiz and crackers."

He had her there. When he sat down and

started eating, she found herself following suit. The truth was, she was entirely too used to eating alone. And she didn't care too much for it, either.

"You want some orange juice?" He got up and went to the fridge, where he pulled out a container of Minute Maid.

"Sure." She took a minute and admired the artwork that was tacked to his refrigerator with a variety of magnets. Shaylee's artwork, no doubt. "It must be hard when she goes back to her mom's."

He glanced up and she indicated the artwork.

Shrugging, he capped the orange juice and put it back in the fridge. "At first it was unbearable. I've adjusted."

She accepted the glass of juice and took a sip. "She seems like a happy kid."

"She is. For the most part. We've had some tough times."

She wasn't sure how much she should push. She figured nobody particularly liked talking about their divorce. Still, she was interested. "Are you and your ex-wife friends?"

He snorted, swallowing a mouthful of eggs. "No. Not really."

She sensed his animosity and didn't push.

"She cheated on me."

The admission didn't exactly surprise her.

She'd figured something had caused the divorce. "That sucks."

"With a woman."

Her eyes grew wide and she chewed carefully. "For real?"

He nodded. "They're currently engaged."

"Wow."

He took a long sip of juice. "I can at least admit the fact now. That's a step in the right direction, according to my brothers."

She couldn't imagine having to deal with a situation like that while having to coparent a child.

"To be honest with you, I've come to the conclusion that I was never as in love with Shelby as I thought I was. Losing her didn't hurt me half as much as losing my right to live with my daughter full time."

"I'm sorry. I saw right away how close you and Shaylee are. She's a great kid."

He smiled a little solemnly. "She is. She's everything to me." He finished off his breakfast. "It's funny. When I first found out Shelby was pregnant I was scared to death. I really didn't think I was the fatherly type. I was basically a kid just out of the military. I was scared all the way up until I held Shaylee in my arms for the first time. At that moment..." His smile grew wider. "At that moment, everything clicked right into place. That's the most in love I've ever felt in my life."

She found herself swallowing hard. The sentiment was about as deep a sentiment as she'd ever heard. "She's lucky to have you."

"I'm lucky to have her." He gathered their dishes and carried them to the sink. "So tell me about your family. Do they live around here?"

"I have a brother up in Washington. He works search and rescue on Rainier."

"No kidding? That would be a great job."

"Adrenaline is Reid's thing. He loves climbing. He's gone on more expeditions than I can count."

"Older or younger?"

"He's four years older."

"Any other brothers or sisters?"

"No. My dad died when I was nine. My mother was gone nine years later. Reid and I have always taken care of each other. He's the reason I joined the military. He was army, too."

He finished loading the dishes into the dishwasher. "My brothers and I were the same way. Drew enlisted first. Slade followed. I'm more of a thinker but it didn't take me long."

"What made you all decide to join different branches?"

He offered her more coffee and she accepted, no longer in such a hurry to go back up to her empty apartment.

He refilled his own cup and gestured to the living room couch.

She got up and followed him, making herself comfortable on one end and wrapping herself up in her blanket.

"As you know, we're triplets," he began, sitting at the opposite end. "We grew up pretty much inseparable. But that ran its course. We needed our own identities and the military gave that to us. For the first time, I wasn't mistaken for anyone else."

"I bet you missed them."

He snorted. "Maybe a little. But don't tell them that. They've both got huge egos."

She laughed at that.

He grew serious after a moment. "Honestly, without those two I wouldn't be here. I had some pretty crazy times during the divorce and no matter how outlandish my behavior got, they reeled me in. They helped me out with Shaylee. They kept me from completely losing my mind. I owe them both."

"I'm sure you've repaid them in some way."

"I don't know about that. They're both pretty squared away. Drew's been in a relationship with his girlfriend Amber for a year now. They're living together and talking about marriage. He's a little slow on the take when it comes to that kind of thing but I know he's in it for the long haul."

"He seems to be happy."

"He is. Amber's good for him. She's been a godsend for Shaylee, too. In a few days, Shaylee's going to hit first grade. Adjusting to a new teacher is going to be a challenge for her."

"I'm sure she'll be okay. She's got a good family background."

"Yeah, I guess she does," he agreed. "She'll have a couple of cousins in April. That gives her something to look forward to."

"Sammy mentioned Slade's girlfriend is pregnant with twins."

"She is. They're planning a small wedding for around Christmas. They just moved in together, too. You've met Bode Cahill, right?"

Mila had met Bode back when she'd met Slade, Drew and Sammy. "I had no idea how entwined you guys all are."

"Just one big, happy family," he agreed.

His phone rang then and he glanced at the device but made no move to answer it.

That felt like a cue so she detangled herself from her blanket and sat up. "I can't believe I've stayed here for so long. What time is it?"

"Just after three." He shrugged his shoulders. "You don't have to take off. It's just my mom. I can call her back in a bit."

Three o'clock! They'd been talking for hours. She immediately stood up. "I have to get back upstairs. I told myself I was going to grocery shop and do laundry today. It's already half over."

"You can thank me for saving you from those boring chores anytime."

She tried not to smile. "Chores like those are necessities. You saw my empty coffee bag."

He laughed and followed her to the door.

She headed into the hallway, her blanket in tow. At the last minute, she turned and faced him. "For real, thank you. For breakfast, I mean. And for the coffee. I was less than human earlier when you knocked on my door. You saved me today."

"I'm sure you'll return the favor at some point. I'm not much better at grocery shopping than you are. Especially when Shaylee's not here."

"I guess I'd better remember that."

He leaned against the doorjamb. "If we both run out of coffee, there's always Mrs. Sherwood on the third floor. She's sixty-five and kind as an old, church lady. But be ready to listen to her life story. She'll talk your ear off if you let her."

"That's good to know. I was wondering about her." She tried to talk herself out of liking him so much. She failed. Clearing her throat, she smiled uneasily. "I should go. Thanks again."

"Sure thing."

She trudged up the stairs, telling herself the whole way that he wasn't that attractive — or charming. He was just a good looking guy who lived downstairs. A good looking guy with a six-year-old and an ex-wife. He'd been around the block. He was definitely not her type.

Repeating that inside her head, she went into her apartment and shut the door behind her with a thud.

5

The first thing Liam did after Mila left was call his mother back.

Debbie Colson, in her mid-sixties, lived across town in the house Liam and his siblings had grown up in. When the triplets were eleven and Jacy was seven, their police officer father had been killed in the line of duty. Debbie had raised all four kids by herself after that. And she'd done a damn good job of it. Liam personally owed her a lot. She'd picked up the slack tremendously when he and Shelby had split up.

"I wondered if I caught you on a shift day," she said in greeting, a minute later.

"No. I was…tied up." He didn't feel like it was the appropriate time to go into detail with his mother about Mila. She would only ask a ton of questions he didn't want to answer. While he liked Mila and knew there was basic interest on his part, he wasn't ready to admit more, even to himself.

"Well I'm surprised your sister hasn't broken down your door."

"Why would she do a thing like that?"

"She's a little upset with me."

Jacy was typically pretty even keeled. She'd gone through a tough time of her own a few months earlier, after trusting the wrong guy. That was what had brought her and Sammy together in the first place, and introduced them to Mila.

"Before you say anything," his mother went on. "Let me explain myself."

He arched a brow. Debbie Colson rarely did anything that caused her to feel the need to explain herself. He figured he'd better sit down, and snatched a seat on the couch. "What's up, Mom?"

"I've been seeing someone."

The words echoed inside his head.

He didn't respond right away and he heard her sigh. "I take it this news is upsetting to you."

It wasn't. Not really. It was just…surprising. To his knowledge, his mother hadn't dated anyone in the past twenty years. At least nobody that she'd allowed her children to know about.

"Liam Daniel. Are you still there?"

He winced at the use of his middle name. "I'm here, Mom. And no, it's not upsetting. Just a little surprising."

"I've seen men over the years."

He winced again. Picturing his mother on dates wasn't something he could easily conjure up.

"I'm going to get to the point because I have a feeling your siblings are going to be pounding on your door at any moment. They're all aware of my situation. While the boys have taken this news far better than Jacy, they're upset with me, too—at least Slade is."

Liam pinched the bridge of his nose. "Okay." He really wasn't sure what he was supposed to say. While it was certainly acceptable for his mother to have a social life, he was a little shocked that this was the first he was hearing of it.

"I'm telling you all this because I'd like you to meet him—the man I've been seeing."

Him. The word echoed back and forth in Liam's head. "Him, who?" he finally found the courage to ask.

"His name is David. David Wallace."

The name didn't ring a bell at all. Curiosity reared its ugly head and he grimaced despite all the rationalizing that tried to take over his thoughts. "Who is this guy?"

"He's a man I met on one of my church retreats."

Over the years, it was no secret that Debbie Colson had remained active in her neighborhood church.

He leaned back against the couch cushions and contemplated the situation. The more he thought about it, the more he wondered why his siblings were making such a big deal out of things. If their mother wanted them to meet her new boyfriend, was that so terrible?

The word *boyfriend* caused him to swallow hard. He had to toss it around a few more times before he was able to come to terms with it. Then he sighed. "I'm good with meeting him, Mom. What's the big deal?"

"You mean that?"

"Sure." A thought occurred to him. "Just how serious are you?"

"I wouldn't be calling you all if I wasn't considering my options here."

He realized pretty quickly that meant *serious.* He expelled a breath and straightened. "Okay. I'll talk to the others."

She didn't respond right away.

"Mom?"

"There is something else," she said quietly.

Before she could finish, someone was

pounding on his front door. He had a pretty good idea who was there. Three guesses covered the possibilities.

"Before you let them in..." she began, obviously having heard the commotion.

He waited for her to finish her sentence.

"Oh never mind. Call me later on when you've calmed down."

"I *am* calm," he responded, frowning at the dial tone that suddenly sounded in his ear. He strolled over and opened the door, expecting to find his sister standing on the stoop.

Jacy was there, along with Slade and Drew. All three of Liam's siblings looked distressed as hell. He stepped back, allowing them room to enter.

"Have you spoken to Mom?" Jacy demanded, not even bothering to remove her jacket.

Liam tossed his phone to the coffee table. "I spoke to her."

"If you spoke with her, why are you so calm?" Slade asked, his eyes narrowed.

Liam kicked the front door shut. "Why shouldn't I be calm? So she's got a boyfriend. Big deal. She's not a nun."

Jacy made a face. "To me she is."

"That's dumb." He walked over to the coffee pot. "You want some?"

"It's mid-afternoon," Slade reminded him.

"I've already had six cups," Drew added.

"No, I don't want coffee," Jacy snapped. "I can't believe you're not upset about this."

Giving up on the coffee, he eyed his sister cautiously. "She's an adult, Jace. She's been alone a long time. Probably mostly for our well-being. I don't think it's so odd that she's looking for companionship. Do you?"

"It's not the companionship that's bothering us," Slade interjected.

Liam folded his arms over his chest and leaned back against the breakfast bar. "Then quit speaking in riddles and tell me what the problem is. Did you run the guy and he's a creep or something?"

"Damn right we ran him," Slade confirmed.

Liam waited for him to say more. He was almost afraid to hear if Slade was this upset. Most things didn't ruffle his youngest brother.

"The guy's forty years old."

Liam stood there stupidly for several seconds until Jacy walked over and snapped her fingers in front of his face. "Did you hear what he said?"

He scowled at her. "Yes, I heard him."

"You realize she's sixty-three."

"I know how old my own mother is."

Jacy flopped down on the couch. "She's Mrs. Robinson."

"She's not married. And he's not twenty-

77

one."

"Forty is the new twenty-one," was all she said.

He muttered an oath and turned to Slade. "What's his story?"

"His story?"

"I mean, did you find out anything bad about him? Does he have a record?"

Slade shrugged. "Not really. A couple of traffic tickets."

"He's a computer programmer, divorced with two grown kids and a grandbaby." This came from Drew, who'd been relatively silent throughout the entire exchange.

"How did you find out all that? You couldn't possibly have done that thorough of a background check already." Even for Drew and Slade, Liam knew there were hoops to jump through for information like that.

Drew shrugged. "Mom told me. Unlike Tweedle Dee and Tweedle Dum here, I listened to her and didn't lose my shit."

"I listened to her," Jacy argued.

"I did, too," Slade agreed.

Drew gave Liam a helpless look.

"You're not upset," Liam figured out. Drew was typically pretty hotheaded so he was a little confused.

"Not really. The guy's not a teenager. Forty

is old enough."

"For our sixty-three-year-old mother? He's only a few years older than we are," Slade exclaimed.

"You're being melodramatic," Drew returned.

"For her to jump right into a relationship with the first man she's dated since Daddy—" Jacy began.

"I think she's dated other men since Dad," Drew interrupted. "She just hasn't flaunted the fact in front of us."

"I was around when you three were in the military. I never saw any men around. She never mentioned any, either." Jacy continued to scowl.

"I think Drew's right," Liam finally said, intervening. "She all but admitted to me today that she's dated off and on over the years. I don't think she's met anyone she's cared about enough until now."

"Why would a forty-year-old man be into a sixty-three-year-old woman?" Slade questioned. "There's got to be something wrong with the guy."

"Well I guess we won't know until we meet him, will we?" Drew pointed out. "And the cop in me tells me we should probably do so as soon as possible."

Liam nodded in agreement.

Begrudgingly, Slade agreed.

Jacy continued to frown.

"You don't have a choice, Jace. And who knows, maybe you'll like the guy." Drew shrugged indifferently. "I think we're all a little old to play the *Daddy* card. He's been gone a long time. She's lonely. We're all living our own lives. She has a right to live hers."

Jacy's expression softened. "When you put it that way…"

Liam could see his sister was coming around. She got up from the couch. "I have to get going. Sammy and I are going to a show tonight. You call mom and set up this meeting. She's pretty mad at me."

"But you'll be there?" Drew questioned.

She rolled her eyes as she headed for the door. "Of course I'll be there."

When she was gone, Liam turned to his brothers. He had something else stuck in his craw, no matter how hard he tried to get it out. "Before you go, I want to ask you something. What do you know about an officer you work with? Ledbetter is his name."

Slade had a blank look on his face.

Drew arched a brow. "Are you talking about Bryan Ledbetter?"

"I don't know his first name. Is there more

than one Ledbetter?"

"Actually, there are a couple—or there were anyway. The older ones retired. Bryan's the youngest—rookie and new to the force. I know this because I did some homework a couple of months ago when Sammy had an issue with him."

This was interesting news. "What happened?"

"Bryan Ledbetter pulled Jacy over for speeding when she was in a precarious situation. She called Sammy to the scene and while he was standing there trying to sort things out, the guy tried to cite her for speeding."

Liam felt his own hackles rise. "You mean during all that Damien Carsen crap?"

Damien Carsen was his sister's ex. Their breakup had been tumultuous, to say the least.

"That's what I mean. Sammy tore the ticket up and all but took the guy's head off. They had words. Ledbetter's a dick from what I've heard. Brubaker worked with him for a while and so did Finley—both recently." Drew shrugged. "Why?"

"Because he's partners with Mila Barnes currently and I saw something this morning that I didn't like." He went on to fill his brothers in on what had happened.

Slade was thoughtful. "She's a good cop. I

saw that firsthand. What's the guy's problem?"

"I get the feeling from her that he's hellbent on letting her know he doesn't appreciate the fact that he has a woman for a partner." The very thought pissed Liam off even more.

"That's illegal," Drew reasoned. "She should report him."

"She's afraid to blacklist herself. She's only been with the bureau for a week." Now that he was coming to Mila's defense, Liam found himself understanding her position a little more.

"If he's pulling crap like that, he's dangerous. She needs to bite the bullet and report him. You're a witness," Drew reasoned.

"I told her to. I don't think she's willing to throw in the towel just yet. She's a pretty tough cookie." He smiled as he thought of the quick moves she'd used on Michael Kendall that morning that had almost taken him down.

"She had some trouble with that asshole back in Eugene," Slade mused. "Winters was his name. You'll have to ask Sammy the details if you want the lowdown. I know that's why she left the EPD."

Liam made a mental note to call Sammy when he had a chance.

"Just how do you know so much about Mila Barnes anyway?" Drew asked, raising an eyebrow. "You got all that from one lousy call you took with her?"

Lying to his brothers wasn't an option. Right then he hated that fact. "We talked a little. She does live upstairs."

"Uh huh," Drew said, grinning like a fool.

"Am I missing something here?" Slade asked, clearly confused.

"I was over the other night and Mila showed up at his door asking for his brute strength in her bedroom." Drew continued to grin.

Slade's own lips quirked. "No kidding?"

"She had a mattress she needed help moving. It was nothing as nefarious as this clown's making it sound," Liam defended indignantly.

"He was gone for almost an hour. It must have been a mighty heavy mattress."

Liam shot Drew a lethal stare. "I told you the other night, I changed the batteries in her smoke detectors before I left. You're such a dick."

Drew just laughed.

Slade grinned in his own right. "She's cute. No exes loitering around that I know of. I can ask Sammy. He'd know."

"Why would I care about that?" Liam asked irritably. "I hardly know the girl."

"You're into her. I can tell." Drew gave Liam a slap on the back that nearly rattled his teeth. "I'm happy for you, bro. It's about time."

"I knew you'd snap out of this Shelby shit

sooner or later," Slade agreed.

"Shut up, both of you!" Liam finally raised his voice. He knew it was the only way to get their attention. As much as he loved them, they were both hard-headed fools. "And don't you dare say a word to anyone at the bureau. She asked me not to involve any of you."

"Calm down," Drew advised. "She is right upstairs."

Finally losing his patience, Liam strode to the door and opened it. "Get out."

Both his brothers grinned like Cheshire cats as they exited the apartment.

6

Once Mila had showered and dressed, she made an attempt to cover the bruise on her jaw with makeup. It had darkened overnight. She was just going to have to deal with the damn thing until it faded.

Sitting down at the table, she made a quick shopping list. Then she grabbed her purse and took off for the grocery store.

One of the reasons she hated grocery shopping was because she was terrible at making decisions when it came to food. Her moods were erratic. She never knew what she was going to want for dinner. She never knew what she was going to crave for lunch. Usually, she wasn't much of a breakfast person at all.

That made purchasing food for an entire week hell.

Pushing her cart, she went up and down the aisles, snatching this and that as she moved. By the time she was finished and her groceries were loaded into the back of her SUV, she was irritable again. Her checking account had taken a fairly good hit. She'd had to buy cleaning supplies and a few things for the apartment that she'd left behind in Eugene.

Just as she was unloading her groceries back at the apartment, a shadow fell across the sidewalk in front of her. "What in the hell is wrong with you?"

She looked up into her brother's angry eyes, surprised. "Reid? What are you doing here?"

"What am I doing here?" He snatched the bags from her arms, clearly upset about something. "I'm here because I've been calling you for days now and you haven't answered your freaking phone!"

"Calm down," she said automatically when his voice raised. They were standing just outside the Victorian and she didn't want to alert the neighbors.

"I will not calm down, Mila. We had a deal. You answer my calls, I leave you be. You didn't keep up your end of the bargain.

She realized he was right. For the past several

days, she'd been so wrapped up in her misery over Ledbetter and her work environment that she'd either been too tired or too busy to talk. She'd meant to return Reid's calls but she hadn't had a day off until now. "I'm sorry," she relented, grabbing the rest of her bags and shutting the hatch on her vehicle. She led him up the walk toward the Victorian. "I've been working the graveyard. You knew that. It was my first week. It's been hectic."

When they reached the top of the stairs and stood in front of her apartment, he waited for her to unlock the door, his six-foot-two frame towering over her from behind.

She set her bags on the counter once they were inside. Then she contemplated how to hide the bruise on her face from him. She knew he was going to go ballistic when he saw it. Hurriedly, she went to work putting away her groceries. "You came a long way just to check in with me. You should have tried to call me today. I'm home now."

"I did try to call you today. Check your messages." He leaned against the breakfast bar silently. She didn't meet his gaze but she knew he was staring at her. "What happened to your face?"

Shit. She tossed a bag of coffee into a nearby cabinet. "Minor injury on the job. It's not a big deal."

He took her by the arm and turned her around, his hazel eyes carefully examining the bruise on her jaw. "Looks like a big deal to me. Some perp tag you?"

"More or less," she responded, not really wanting to go into detail with him. If Reid found out about what was going on with her partner at work...

"Why do I feel like you're hiding something from me?"

His voice cut into her thoughts and she felt like squirming. She'd never been good at lying to him. That was another reason she'd been avoiding his calls all week.

Continuing to put her groceries away, she shrugged. "Because you're paranoid. I'm not hiding anything. And you shouldn't just come here without letting me know. I do have a life of my own."

"Is that right." His deep voice lowered a few notches. "Okay. If that's how you feel, I can leave."

Immediately she backtracked. "No. I'm sorry. I didn't mean that."

"What's going on with you, Mila? You're not taking my calls. You don't look happy to see me at all. You're bruised up and jumpy."

"I'm not jumpy."

"You're jumpy. When I came up to you outside you just about leapt out of your skin."

"You startled me, that's all. You have to admit your approach was less than subtle."

He had the decency to look a little sheepish. "I was pissed. I don't like being ignored. Not by you."

She softened a bit. "I should have called you back sooner. I wasn't ignoring you. I've just been a little stressed. New apartment, new job. It's a lot."

"I realize that." He peered around the disorganized apartment. "You planning to unpack?"

"Eventually."

"I'm here now. I can help."

"I'd rather order pizza and open a beer. We can catch up." She smiled for the first time since he'd arrived. "What do you say? Can you stay the night?"

"Oh I'm staying the night. I've got a bag in the car. I do have to head home tomorrow. I'm on call Sunday."

"Then let's get to it."

· · ·

Liam spent his weekend off taking care of some much-needed chores. He did a few loads of laundry and re-stocked his pantry for when Shaylee returned to his place the following Friday. Then he changed the oil in his truck—something he'd been putting off for a while.

Mechanics was somewhat of a hobby for him. As a young kid, he'd watched his dad—a car buff—tinker with vehicles all the time. Now he found himself doing the same thing. Fortunately, there was enough room for him to work out in front of the Victorian.

Just as he was cleaning up his mess, he caught sight of Mila exiting the house, a tall man behind her with a duffel bag in his hand. Liam hadn't seen her since Friday afternoon when she'd left his apartment.

Wiping his hands on a rag, he observed the two curiously.

"Hey," she said, smiling as she reached the sidewalk.

He tossed his rag aside and smiled back. "Hey."

The man behind her was tall with dark hair. He wasn't smiling or frowning. He was just staring at Liam with interest. Liam immediately got a strange vibe off the guy.

"Liam Colson, Reid Barnes. Liam is my neighbor downstairs," she went on to explain. "Reid is my older brother."

Liam automatically held out his hand.

"How's it going?" the man greeted, shaking it.

He still seemed a bit aloof but Liam ignored the attitude. Now that he knew this was her sibling, he figured it was an overprotective brother thing. He'd exhibited the same attitude himself with a few of Jacy's male friends.

"Not bad. You?"

"I can't complain. You a mechanic?"

Liam shook his head. "Not really. I work for the fire department. I tinker with cars in my spare time."

"Good to know. That relic she drives could use a tune up."

"My vehicle is fine," she said, shooting her brother a warning look. "Shouldn't you be getting on the road? You have a long drive ahead of you."

He shot a look back in her direction, then pulled his keys from his pocket and gave Liam a polite nod. "It was nice to meet you."

"You, too."

Liam watched as the pair walked half a block down the street where her brother hit the locks and opened the door of a red Chevy truck.

"Excuse me?" a man's voice said from behind Liam.

He turned. He'd been so absorbed in his observation of Mila and Reid Barnes that he hadn't noticed a florist van drive up and park behind his truck. He eyed the large bouquet of flowers the man carried. "Can I help you?"

"Maybe. I'm looking for Mila Barnes. This is the address I was given. Am I in the right place?"

He examined the large bouquet of colorful blooms. They were tasteful. Expensive. Clearly a gesture to get her attention.

He frowned, suddenly more annoyed than he wanted to be. Who in the hell was sending her flowers? Slade had specifically said she didn't have any boyfriends, hadn't he?

He thought back to the conversation he'd had with his brother. In all actuality, if he recalled correctly, Slade hadn't known for sure. He'd mentioned the idea of asking Sammy.

"I'm running a little behind today," the delivery guy said, shifting the bouquet into his other hand. He sounded a little annoyed now. "Am I in the right place?"

Liam couldn't exactly deny it. "You are," he eventually admitted. "I know her. You can leave the flowers with me."

The guy looked a little skeptical but when his cell phone rang, he sighed in frustration and handed the flowers over. "The card's in there."

Liam felt the sudden urge to dig around in the arrangement until he found the card so he could see just who it was she was getting flowers from. His conscience told him it was none of his business. He hardly knew her. And she hardly knew him. It wasn't likely that she'd appreciate him snooping into her business.

"Somebody likes you an awful lot." She was there suddenly, in front of him on the sidewalk. She was observing the flowers with amusement in her dark eyes.

Knowing he had no choice, he shook his head. "They're not mine. They're yours."

She arched a brow. "You shouldn't have."

He offered the arrangement to her. "I didn't. The card's inside somewhere."

Obviously surprised, she accepted the flowers, her nose immediately buried in the blooms.

He leaned back against his truck and watched her for a moment. Suddenly he wished he had sent her the flowers. They seemed to be making her happy.

"Who dropped them off?" she asked, meeting his gaze.

"Some delivery guy. He was in a hurry so I told him I'd make sure they ended up in the right place."

"Thank you." She dug through the greenery until she found a small, pink card. Balancing the flowers on her hip, she managed to dig the card out of the envelope.

As she read, her expression darkened. He immediately took notice. "You okay?"

She scowled and crumpled up the card. "Where is the garbage around here?"

Intrigued, he pointed to the alley behind the house. "Out back. There's a Dumpster we share."

She marched around the side of the house. When she returned, the flowers were not with her.

Arching a brow of his own, he snorted. "Trouble in paradise?"

"I'm not sure what kind of paradise you're referring to."

"Unless you sent yourself flowers and pissed yourself off, someone else did." The idea that she might have a boyfriend crossed his mind again. On the other hand, if she did, she certainly didn't appear happy to hear from the guy — flowers or not.

She offered him the crumpled, pink envelope. "Go ahead and read it."

A little surprised, he accepted the envelope and slid the card from inside.

"Mila, I'm sorry we got off on the wrong foot this week. Let's start fresh. I'll buy you dinner. Let me know. Bryan."

"Bryan," he repeated out loud.

"Ledbetter," she clarified, scowling.

"You're shitting me." He slid the card back inside its envelope and frowned.

"No. He's the only Bryan I know who would say something like that to me."

Snorting, he handed the card back. So now the jerk was backtracking. Interesting.

"I don't know why he'd send me flowers. He clearly hates me."

He had his doubts about that. "Maybe he doesn't hate you as much as you think he does." The idea was annoying and he worked at keeping his voice neutral.

"He does. He practically let me get my ass kicked multiple times."

"Multiple times?" Anger spiked and he found himself wanting to kick the crap out of Bryan Ledbetter himself.

"Never mind." She continued to scowl at the card. "He knows people witnessed his poor performance on the job yesterday. He's worried about me telling Tennant. That's the only explanation."

He supposed that was a possibility. Secretly happy that she'd thrown the flowers out, he considered her again. "You really should file a report. The guy's an asshole."

"We've been over this. What are you doing tonight?"

Caught off guard, he just stared at her dumbly.

"Do you have plans?" she asked, rephrasing her question.

Gathering his wits about him, he shook his head. "Shaylee's with her mom until next weekend. Why?"

"You want to go to a movie?"

Dumbfounded again, he just stared at her.

"If you're busy, or if you have a girlfriend, just say so. It's no big deal. There's a movie I want to see and I'm not usually pathetic enough to go to the theater by myself—although I have to admit I have in the past."

"Are you asking me out on a date?" The question was out before he could stop it.

She shrugged and nodded. "I guess. I mean in a way. It doesn't have to be a "date" per say. I don't expect you to pay. I'm asking you."

"You're not paying my way." He was mildly offended.

"Okay. We can go Dutch."

"You're not paying your way, either. If we go to a movie, I'll take care of the paying."

"That's a bit chauvinistic."

"Call me old school."

After a moment, she nodded. "Okay. So are you asking me out then?"

He couldn't help but chuckle at her forward

nature. "You might be the most interesting woman I've ever met."

"Is that a compliment?"

"Yeah, I suppose it is. What movie do you want to see?"

"Julia Roberts and George Clooney have a new flick out. Do you like romcoms?"

"I can tolerate them. I like Clooney. You want to have dinner first?"

"After. If I eat dinner first I won't have room for popcorn. Are you done with your truck?"

He'd almost forgotten about his vehicle. "Pretty much. I need to go clean up though. Give me thirty minutes."

She nodded and walked toward the house. He couldn't help but watch her go, still a little surprised at what had unfolded. She'd asked him out on a date. Or had he asked her? He really wasn't sure anymore.

Gathering his tools together, he headed for his apartment to take a shower.

7

Mila changed into a pair of dark colored jeans and a V-neck sweater her brother had given her for Christmas the year before. It was a nice beige color that brought out the brown in her eyes — or so Reid kept telling her anyway.

After pulling on a pair of knee-high, brown boots, she curled her hair and applied enough makeup to make the bruise on her face almost non-existent.

When she was finished, she admired herself in the mirror for a moment. She looked decent, she decided. Not like she was trying too hard, yet stylish and well put together.

There was a part of her that couldn't believe she'd asked Liam Colson out on a date. She'd never done anything so reckless in her life. And on a total whim. She hadn't thought whatsoever before she'd asked him to take her to a movie. She'd seen him standing there by his truck, his jeans old and dirty, his T-shirt stained with oil and hugging him in all the right places—and decided he was hotter than hell. Her libido had acted for her at that point.

He hadn't seemed too uncomfortable, which was a relief. The whole thing could have been very embarrassing if he'd turned her down. For all she knew, he could have a girlfriend. He hadn't mentioned one but…

A knock sounded on her door and she hesitated. She really didn't know much about the man. Maybe he was a player.

Another knock sounded.

Exhaling, she walked over and opened the door. The sight of him on her stoop silenced her immediately. He'd cleaned up alright. He had fresh jeans and a flannel shirt on. The jacket he wore was a dark blue North Face. His hair was neatly gelled and she noticed immediately that he smelled delicious. Spicy and citrusy.

"You ready?" he asked, jingling his keys in his hand.

"You don't have a girlfriend, do you?"

He narrowed his gaze. "Do you really think I'd be here right now if I did?"

"Maybe. Some guys are tools that way."

He snorted. "Well, I'm not. If you've changed your mind about going out, it's okay. We can skip it."

"No, I haven't. I just realized I pretty much submarined you. I don't know a lot about you. I should have asked about your…status."

"I'm divorced. You already knew that. Should I be concerned that you have a boyfriend?"

She reached for the jacket she'd tossed on a nearby chair earlier. "No. I'm not a tool, either."

"That's good to know." He reached for the jacket and surprised her by holding it up so she could slide her arms into it. When she was safely snuggled inside and zipped, he shook his head at her. "Something tells me you're going to keep me on my toes."

"Is that a compliment, too?"

"I don't know. Ask me at the end of the night."

She found herself grinning. "Will do."

After locking up, she followed him to his truck. The drive to the theater didn't take long, maybe fifteen minutes. True to his word, he paid for their tickets. He also paid for popcorn and drinks.

The movie was a good, tropical flick about a couple whose daughter was getting married. It was amusing and easy to follow. He seemed to enjoy it himself. Either that or he was a good actor.

When it was over, he suggested they grab a bite to eat at a nearby restaurant. She agreed without hesitation. Being with him was easy enough and she was in no hurry to go back to her apartment and sit alone.

When they were seated in a cozy booth near a bank of windows, had ordered some food and each had a beer in hand, she considered him. "How much did you hate the movie?"

"I didn't hate it." He slid his jacket off and set it on the seat next to him. "I'm not going to lie to you and tell you I wouldn't have preferred a Jason Statham flick, but it held my interest."

"I love romcoms. But I can handle a Jason Statham flick, too. I like action."

"Obviously, judging by your profession and some of your life choices." He took a long sip of his beer. "How the hell did you learn how to take a guy down that way anyway? I mean the way you did with Michael Kendall."

She bristled at the memory.

"Sorry. I didn't mean to sour your mood."

"You didn't. I just get mad all over again when I think about what happened." Taking a sip of her own beer, she shrugged her shoulders. "You met my brother today. He taught me self-defense when I was twelve. Karate. He's a blackbelt. I got all the way to brown before I quit and joined the army. I learned a few more moves there — and at the academy."

"I'll have to remember not to piss you off."

She chuckled at that. "You had some pretty good moves yourself. Military?"

He nodded. "Both of my brothers were Special Forces."

"Impressive. That takes dedication."

"Yeah. I thought about the SEAL thing. Not for long. I knew I wasn't career military."

"Because of the medicine thing," she remembered aloud.

"Yeah. And like you said, the dedication thing. I just knew I wanted to do other stuff. Not to bring up bad tidings but once Shaylee came along, I knew I couldn't be gone all the time. After losing my dad at such a young age…" He lifted one shoulder. "I just didn't want my daughter to grow up without me around."

"That must have been hard, losing your dad so young."

"It was. He was killed in the line of duty."

She winced. "How awful. Your poor mom. Four kids and on her own."

"The police department made sure we were taken care of financially. And my dad had friends who were very dedicated to seeing us through the tough times. It was a rough adjustment though."

"Like I told you, my parents are both dead. My brother and I have always been tight. He's my knight in shining armor."

He grinned. "Yeah, I got that protective vibe off him today. I don't think he was real happy to see me at first."

"Probably not. He would definitely prefer my neighbors were female."

"In other words, he wouldn't be pleased if he knew we're together right now."

"I'm probably not going to tell him," she admitted. "He can be nosy and overbearing. As much as I love him, I like to make my own decisions without interference from him."

"I hear you. My brothers and sister are the same way. I went a few rounds with them this morning."

"About what?"

He seemed a little uncomfortable at first. Eventually he relaxed. "My mother has a boyfriend."

She wasn't sure if she was supposed to act surprised or not, so she just waited for him to say more.

"He's forty."

"Okay." She frowned. "Is that a bad thing?"

"She's sixty-three."

She immediately caught on. "Ah."

"She's never so much as brought a man home over the past twenty years. I had no idea she was even dating."

"Your dad's been gone a long time," she replied as gently as she could. "My mom was dating a year after my dad died."

"Didn't that bother you?"

She thought that over. "Maybe for a while at first. But I figured out pretty quickly that she was lonely and the less lonely she was, the more she stayed out of my business. Smart teenager thinking." She winked at him and he laughed.

Their food arrived and she dug into her hamburger enthusiastically. Despite the popcorn she'd eaten, she was starving.

He'd ordered the same thing and he began eating, too.

"So have you met this guy?" she asked curiously a few minutes later.

"No. I only found out about him this morning. My sister is mortified. Slade isn't too far behind her. Drew is always the peacemaker. He's just trying to put out all the fires this has started."

"I know forty seems young but if she likes the man enough to introduce him to you guys, maybe he's the real deal. Sometimes love is blind."

He took a drink of his beer. "Yeah, I've

thought about that. But it is a little unnerving that the guy is only eight years older than I am."

She dipped a French fry in ketchup. "I guess I can understand that. So what are you going to do?"

"There's not much I can do. Drew and Slade have already checked him out. They haven't found any red flags." He wiped his mouth with a napkin. "If I know Slade, he's still looking. The fact of the matter is, Mom's an adult. She's always been a pretty good judge of character. I reserve the right to change my mind until I've met the man though. If he's a dick..."

She grinned. "Like you just said, if she's a good judge of character, he probably won't be."

"Let's hope not."

They finished their meals and he paid the bill. The entire way back to the Victorian, the conversation flowed easily. He parked in his spot and they walked inside together. When they were at her door, she turned, giving him a grateful smile. "You're a good sport. Thank you for going along with this. I wasn't in the mood to sit home alone tonight."

He leaned against the wall nearby, his gray eyes searching hers. "I didn't *go along* with anything. I was thinking about asking you out anyway."

"You were?"

He shrugged and nodded. "I'm a little out of practice with this stuff. I haven't been on a lot of dates since the divorce."

"It's like riding a bike, right?"

His lips quirked. "Yeah, I guess it is. If you're with the right person anyway."

They stood there silently for several seconds before he finally lowered his head and their noses bumped. At that point, she closed the distance between them and her mouth covered his.

The kiss was light, fleeting at first. Before too long, she opened. Their tongues slid together almost immediately and she lost all train of thought. There was no arguing with the fact that this man knew how to kiss. And he tasted like a little piece of heaven.

They stood there for a while, each enjoying what the other had to offer. Eventually, he lifted his head, his fingers framing her face. "It's getting late. I should go."

She backed up, giving him a little space. "I really did have a good time tonight. Thank you again."

"You're welcome. We'll do this again. I get to pick the movie."

"Only if I get to pay."

He shook his head. "Sorry, sweetheart. Like I said, I'm old school. I'll see you." He was already heading down the stairs.

She stared after him until he disappeared around the corner. Then she went into her apartment and shut the door. Without conscious thought, she lifted her fingers to her lips. Before she knew it, she was smiling. After one hell of a bad week, things were finally looking up.

8

By Sunday night, Mila was counting down the minutes until she had to head to work. It was all she could do to choke down some dinner, swallow a mug of coffee and drag herself out to her vehicle.

The bruise on her face still looked rough but she'd managed to cover it for the most part. She was getting to be a whiz with make-up.

She glanced at Liam's closed door as she walked past his apartment. All was quiet. It was half past eleven in the evening so he was most likely sleeping. She hadn't seen him since their impromptu date on Saturday night. She'd spent Sunday doing laundry, paying bills and going through boxes. She hadn't ventured out of her apartment at all.

Truthfully, she was after nothing but a little companionship herself — a little fun. A periodic distraction from her day-to-day struggle. She sensed he wasn't into anything heavy, either. His ex-wife had put him through the wringer and he was definitely skittish.

Perhaps they were both on the same page.

Settling herself in the driver's seat, she shoved the key in the ignition and turned. All she received for her efforts was a click.

Giving it another try, she grimaced when the same thing happened.

She was suddenly reminded of her brother's warning that her vehicle needed some work. She was pretty good about getting the oil changed. She usually managed to get the SUV serviced every few-thousand miles, as recommended.

She glanced at the small sticker in the upper left-hand corner of the windshield. Frowning, she realized it had been a bit longer than she'd thought. In all the chaos of the move, she'd missed her oil change appointment. The vehicle was a thousand miles overdue.

Frustrated, she tried one last time to get the SUV to start. Still, only a click sounded.

Yanking the key from the ignition, she peered at her cell phone for the time. She only had fifteen minutes to get to the precinct or she would be late for her shift.

Admitting defeat, she contemplated her options. She could call the precinct and let them know she was having car trouble. Under normal circumstances, it wouldn't be that big of a deal to have her partner pick her up at home this one time. Then she would be able to call a garage and get the car worked on.

Under normal circumstances. She repeated the phrase inside her head several times. She definitely didn't have those. Not with Ledbetter involved. This would only give him more ammunition in his vendetta against her.

She brought up her Uber app, praying there was a car in the area that could pick her up quickly.

No such luck. The nearest driver was twenty minutes out. Cursing, she gave up and grabbed her bag. After locking up the SUV, she went back to the Victorian. She hesitated in front of Liam's door. He was really her only other option.

Taking a deep breath, she knocked.

She heard shuffling after a minute and eventually the door opened.

Liam stood before her, wearing a pair of pajama pants and a T-shirt. His hair was sleep-mussed and his feet were bare. When he realized it was her on the doorstep, he frowned. "What's wrong?"

She didn't have time for preliminary conversation so she just filled him in immediately. "I'm sorry to wake you. My car won't start. I have fifteen minutes to get to work or my ass is grass. I don't suppose if I promise you the world, you could help me out."

He stared at her for a moment. "What's wrong with your car?"

"If I knew, I wouldn't be standing here. It just won't start."

He scratched his head and let out a sigh. "Okay. Hang on a second. Let me change." He left the door open and disappeared down the hallway. When he returned a couple of minutes later, he was fully dressed in jeans and a sweatshirt. He even had his shoes on. Obviously his time at the firehouse had trained him to move quickly at a moment's notice.

"Is it making any noise at all?" he asked, stepping into the hall.

"Just a clicking noise." She led the way out to the street.

"It might be your battery. I can give you a jump if you want. I have cables. Or I can just give you a ride, but you'll be stuck. I have to be at work at seven AM."

She glanced at her watch again. Another five minutes had passed. There was really no way to reach the precinct in time anyway. "I'm sorry. I hate to bother you this way."

"It's not a big deal, Mila. What do you want to do?"

"We should probably try the jump thing. I'll call the precinct while you pull your truck around."

He nodded and disappeared.

She phoned in and left a message with the person who answered the phone. Ledbetter wasn't in yet.

Liam pulled around and parked in front of her vehicle. Fortunately, there was room. It didn't take him long to hook up the jumper cables. Five minutes later, her engine rumbled to life.

She exhaled a sigh of relief. "Thank you!"

"No worries. How old is your battery?"

"I don't remember exactly. Old, I guess."

"I'd be careful about turning the engine off right away. The battery may go dead again. If it's the alternator, that's a whole different issue."

She tossed her stuff into the vehicle again. "Will do. Thank you again. I owe you. So much for me not being indebted to you."

He disconnected the jumper cables and considered her. "I'm not keeping track, Mila. We're friends. If I can help you out, I will. You want me to follow you to work in case you have another problem?"

"I'll be fine. It's not that far."

"Give me your phone."

"Huh?" She stared at him dumbly.

He took the phone from her fingers and punched in some numbers. Then he handed it back to her. "So you can call me if you have trouble. We should have exchanged numbers before anyway. We are neighbors. Just text me when you get a chance and I'll have yours."

She nodded and hopped into her vehicle. Another glance at the time had her grimacing. She was ten minutes late. Cursing, she threw the vehicle into gear and hit the gas.

Her bad luck continued. When she got to the precinct, she ran into Tennant on her way inside the building. It was after midnight. Normally he worked during the day shift. It just figured the one time she was late he would be in the building.

He gave her face a quick onceover. "Barnes. You're looking better."

"I am better, sir," she stammered.

"Shifts start on the hour here. Make sure you're on time in the future." That was it. He walked away.

Sighing in frustration, she hurried to her locker and deposited her things. By the time she stepped out back where she knew Ledbetter would be waiting at their patrol car, she was flustered and aggravated.

"What's wrong with your car?" Ledbetter asked as she approached. "Anything I can help you with?"

She'd braced herself for the worst. This was not what she'd been expecting. Clearing her throat, she decided not to look a gift horse in the mouth. "It's the battery. I've got it handled, thanks. Sorry I'm late."

He shrugged. "Things are quiet so far."

They climbed into their patrol car and settled in for their shift. About twenty minutes into patrol, he glanced at her. "Aren't you going to say anything?"

Confused, she arched a brow. "About what?"

"Didn't you get the flowers?"

She bristled. She'd almost forgotten about those. "Oh, yes, I got them. Thanks."

He frowned. "Were they not nice? They set me back a hundred bucks."

Even when he was trying to be nice he came across like a jerk. Ignoring that fact, she forced a smile, determined to keep the peace. "They were nice. I would have gotten around to thanking you. I've had a hectic start tonight."

"I can take a look at your car. I'm handy enough with a wrench. I used to work on cars in my spare time in high school."

"It's okay. My neighbor already looked at it. He's pretty sure it's the battery. I'll grab a new one tomorrow."

"I can put it in for you."

The nicer he got, the more skeptical she became. What was this sudden change in attitude about? Last week he'd treated her like dirt. Now he was sending her flowers and trying to be her best friend.

She supposed it was best to accept his sudden change of heart, whatever the reason. "I appreciate the offer but I can handle it. It's just a battery."

"Suit yourself."

They did their rounds, then stopped for coffee. Just as they were getting back into the patrol car, a call came over dispatch. A suspected burglary.

Ledbetter headed that direction.

The address was about ten minutes from their location, in a middle-class neighborhood not too far from the river. When they arrived on the scene, they found the house was well-lit. The front door stood open. There was a small crowd gathered in the foyer when Mila tapped her knuckles against the doorjamb.

"Come in!" a woman exclaimed, glancing their way. "Thank goodness you're here!"

Mila stepped into the entry way, Ledbetter on

her heels. She identified them both.

The woman introduced herself as Claire Whitfield. She was fifty-two years old and shared the home with her two children, Mark and Jana. Also on the scene were a pair of neighbors.

Apparently, Claire had been out for the evening and so had her eighteen-year-old-son. When she'd returned home, she'd found her daughter huddled up on the couch, upset. She'd tried getting a story out of the sixteen-year-old but the girl had been traumatized and hysterical.

Just looking around the room, Mila could see there had been a struggle. There was broken glass littering the floor and a lamp was upended. In the far corner of the room, a young girl was huddled on the couch, a blanket wrapped around her.

"What does she say happened?" Mila asked the mother quietly.

"It was hard to make sense of what she was saying. She was so upset." The woman was clearly upset in her own right. She took a couple of deep breaths. "She mentioned someone coming in through the back door. It's a slider off the kitchen. It should have been locked. I checked it before I left the house. I just don't understand how this happened."

"Where was your son?" Mila asked.

"At work. He's a driver for Stefano's Pizza. He works until midnight. He got home about twenty minutes after I did."

"I'll talk to the girl," Ledbetter said, already stepping around Mila. Before she could stop him, he headed across the room toward the teenager.

Mila's instincts kicked in. Ledbetter didn't have the best bedside manner, so to speak. He was rough around the edges and matter of fact. It was all she could do not to argue with him.

Instead of acting on the urge, she turned to Mark Whitfield, a tall, gangly kid with a head of dark hair and a scruffy beard. She asked him several routine questions, which he answered.

After she was done there, she joined Ledbetter, who was sitting on the couch near Jana Whitfield.

The girl was blond and small, probably not much taller than Mila, who was a couple of inches over five feet. She was still huddled under her blanket. There were tear streaks running down her face and her mascara was smeared underneath both eyes.

"I'm Officer Barnes," Mila said, taking a seat not far from Ledbetter. "You're Jana, right?"

The girl nodded.

"She's answered all my questions. Perp came in through the back door. She was in the family room watching a movie and he caught her by surprise." Ledbetter looked at the teen. "Isn't that right?"

The girl nodded solemnly.

"Did he hurt you?" Mila asked automatically. She could see a bruise forming on the girl's left cheek.

"She says no," Ledbetter answered before the teenager had the chance.

When Mila's eyes locked with Jana Whitfield's, she got a very strange vibe from the girl. She got the feeling that there was more going on here than met the eye. "Are you sure?" she prodded. "What happened to your face?"

"I fell. I tripped over the lamp."

"Are you hurt anywhere else?"

The girl hesitated.

Mila had dealt with situations like this before. She had a very bad feeling suddenly. "Would it be easier if you spoke with me alone?"

Ledbetter shot her an elbow. She ignored it.

The girl eventually shook her head.

"Jana, you can tell us anything. We're here to help," Mila encouraged. "Do you need an ambulance?"

"I—I don't think so." She peered toward the hallway where her mother and brother were still standing, both with concerned expressions on their faces. "I'm okay. Just rattled. Can I go

118

upstairs now?" The teenager was on her feet suddenly.

Ledbetter stood, too. "We'll photograph the scene. Can you make us a list of what's missing?" He was already heading off toward Mrs. Whitfield.

Mila knew something was off. She reached for Jana's arm at the last minute, once she was certain Ledbetter was gone. "Were you sexually assaulted?"

The girl's eyes grew wide. "No! I told you, I'm fine!"

"If you were—"

"I told Officer Ledbetter everything already. Just leave me alone." The kid disappeared up the stairs.

Ledbetter shot Mila a look from across the room that told her she was way out of bounds. She kept her expression impassive for the sake of the Whitfield family.

Against her better judgement, she let Ledbetter take the lead. Eventually it was determined that a small amount of cash was missing from the home, along with some jewelry. The crime scene was photographed.

Mila left a business card with Mrs. Whitfield when Ledbetter turned his back, even though he'd already left one. She just couldn't shake the bad feeling she had. "If your daughter thinks of anything else, just have her give me a call. Sometimes once a person calms down, they remember something they forgot to mention initially that might help in an investigation."

Claire Whitfield took the card. "She's so upset. I've never seen her this way."

It was on the tip of Mila's tongue to tell the woman her thoughts.

"Barnes! Let's go!" Ledbetter called from the front walk. He was already almost to the patrol car.

Masking her annoyance, Mila forced a sympathetic smile for Mrs. Whitfield. "She's scared. She's been through a traumatic experience. See how she's doing in the morning. And use that card if you need to. Anytime. My cell number is on there."

Mrs. Whitfield nodded and Mila left the residence. Once she was back in the vehicle, she turned to Ledbetter, who, unconcerned, was already starting up the engine. "What did that girl say to you before I joined the conversation?"

He straightened. "I told you what she said. A man broke in through the back slider. He had a gun. He took money and went through the house. He scared the hell out of her."

"I think he may have done more than that," she said, buckling her seatbelt.

"You mean rape?"

The word echoed throughout the vehicle and she nodded.

"She didn't mention anything about a sexual assault."

"She's scared to death," Mila reasoned. "And you're a man."

"What's that got to do with it? I'm a policeman."

"She's a kid, Ledbetter. A *traumatized* kid. You should have let me take the lead."

Something flickered in those dark eyes of his and he glared at her. "Are you insinuating I don't know how to do my job?"

Just like that, they were back on unstable ground.

Sighing, she shook her head. "That's not what I'm saying at all. I just think in certain cases where sexual assault is suspected, it's easier for a female victim to speak to a female officer."

"I didn't suspect sexual assault," he argued, making no move to pull out into traffic.

"Well, I did. I tried to get your attention but you took charge before I had the chance to discuss the matter with you. That girl did not tell the entire story of what happened tonight. She had bruises. There were signs of a struggle."

"That doesn't mean shit," he snapped. "And it was a bruise. Not multiple. She explained how she got it."

"Did you examine the rest of her body for other injuries?" she countered, keeping her eyes locked with his. She was done bowing down to this jerk.

His jaw clenched. "Obviously not. That would have been uncalled for. She's just a kid and I'm a guy."

He'd just proved her point for her. She remained silent.

He muttered a string of curses and finally pulled out into the street. "You're way out of bounds here, Barnes."

"We're supposed to be working together, Ledbetter. That's the idea of a partnership. That's what makes a partnership successful. The possibility of two different perspectives."

"I saw you question her yourself before we left. She denied it."

That was true. But Mila couldn't help but feel if she'd started the interview with the kid herself, they'd be sitting on an entirely different scenario right now. "Just forget it. What's done is done. I left my card. If she wants to talk, she'll call me."

"Whatever." Ledbetter was silent the entire way back to the precinct. They wrote up a report and filed it before heading back out on the beat. The rest of their shift, thankfully, was uneventful. By the time it ended that morning, she had a splitting headache. As if things weren't bad enough, when she went to start her vehicle, the damn thing was dead again. Yanking her phone from her purse, she scrolled through it in search of the nearest auto parts store.

9

Liam went on shift at seven that morning. Station 41 was in the heart of downtown. He had been with the department for several years now.

"You're on dinner tonight, Colson."

Liam shut his locker and glanced up. Cain Cruz stood in the doorway, a clipboard in his hand.

Cruz, blond haired and blue-eyed, reminded Liam of a California surfer. A couple of years younger than Liam, he had just started with the department a few months earlier.

"Okay, I'll take care of it." Everyone at the station had dinner duty during the month. It was a way for each of them to have a decent meal if shifts were slow.

"We've got a grocery list. Have fun."

Liam grimaced at the thought of going to the grocery store. Accepting the list, he was glad to note it consisted of something simple. The fixings for Spaghetti. He could handle that.

He went in search of his good friend, Travis Scott. He and his buddy usually carried out this task together.

Travis, recently promoted to captain, and Liam had hit it off the moment they'd started working together. At thirty-three, Travis had also been through a divorce. He had no children but he and his ex had still navigated the tumultuous waters of a nasty break up.

Travis was no worse for the wear. He'd jumped right back into the dating game and had a pretty active social circle that he was always trying to include Liam in. Not only that, he and his ex-wife were friends now—something Liam himself couldn't imagine with his own situation.

Travis was tall with brown hair and light blue eyes. He was a gym rat, always concerned about keeping himself in good shape. He and Liam worked out together now and then.

The two rounded up their squad and headed for the store. They always went in a group. It wasn't unheard of for a call to come in while they were shopping, giving them no choice but to leave their cart behind.

While the other guys waited outside, Travis and Liam went into the supermarket.

"How are things with Shelby?" Travis asked, tossing several boxes of pasta into the cart.

"Same," Liam replied, tackling a few items on the list himself.

"Meaning you're still not speaking."

"We speak. When we have to."

Travis leaned on the cart, his eyes narrowed. "The longer you drag this out, the more you're hurting yourself, and Shaylee. You know that, right?"

"I don't need the lecture. My family has that covered."

"So go out with me tomorrow night. We'll hit a club. I met this hot stewardess last weekend. She's got friends. I'll do some recon and set you up. Or if you don't like that, I'll talk to Sloan and see if she can wrangle up somebody at the hospital. There are always new prospects there."

Sloan Wyatt was a good friend of Travis's that Liam had met several times. She was a nurse at Portland General so he also knew her through Ella. She was married to a fellow firefighter, Justin Wyatt. He worked out of a different station but he and Liam crossed paths occasionally.

He was shaking his head before he even thought about it.

"You need to get back on the horse, Colson. It's been months."

"Again, you sound like my family." He thought about Mila. Had he already gotten back on the horse? She definitely had his interest. When she'd driven off to work the night before, he'd been worried enough about her car to shoot her a text halfway through the night. She'd answered politely, putting his mind at ease.

Were they just friends?

He thought about the kiss they'd shared after their "date" the other night.

His skin heated up instantly.

"Okay, what gives?"

Liam met his friend's curious gaze, a little startled at the path his thoughts had taken. "What are you talking about?"

"You didn't jump my ass when I suggested you get back on the horse. Are you already back on it?"

Liam thought about that. Again, he was confused. He knew he liked Mila — more than he'd liked any woman since he'd split up with Shelby.

The thing was, she had an air about her. He got the feeling she wasn't into anything serious — not that he was either at this point. They really didn't know each other that well.

"Spill. If you're thinking this hard, you're

definitely back on the horse."

Liam frowned. "I don't know that I want to talk about it yet. It may be nothing."

Travis threw a few more items into the cart. "Like I said, if you're thinking about it this hard—"

"Okay, okay," Liam relented. "I met someone. Actually, she moved in upstairs from me."

"You mean in Amber's apartment?"

Liam nodded.

"Well, who is she?"

Liam hesitated again.

"Wait a minute. You're not talking about the cop. The one you rescued the other day."

Travis was very good at connecting the dots. Nothing got past him. Liam shrugged and nodded. "We went out Saturday night. It wasn't planned. It just kind of happened."

Travis laughed. "She's a little fireball."

Liam couldn't deny it.

"So what gives? If she finally got you to come out of your shell and ask her out, you must be interested."

Liam didn't really want to admit Mila had been the one to ask him out. He knew Travis was going to rib him.

"Don't tell me *she* asked *you* out." Travis continued to laugh.

"Why is that such a big deal?" Liam asked irritably.

Travis sobered a little. "It's not. Not really. It's just funny. I know you too well."

Liam flipped him a subtle gesture so nobody else saw.

Unaffected, Travis prodded on. "So how did it go?"

Liam went to work unloading groceries when they got to the checkout counter. "It was fine."

"Fine." Travis folded his arms over his chest and grinned again. "That's not very promising."

"We went to a movie and out to dinner. Nothing too monumental."

"Did she pay?" Travis's grin widened.

Again, Liam shot him a rude gesture. "Of course not. I'm not a total loser."

Travis pulled out his credit card when their purchases had been added up. "Well do you like her or not?"

"I wouldn't have even gone out with her if I didn't. But it's complicated. I'm not in the best place mentally. She just moved here. She's got a lot going on at work." Liam shrugged.

Travis took their receipt. "I noticed her partner is a dick. That sucks for her."

"Yeah, he sent her flowers."

"No shit?"

Liam pushed the cart toward the exit. "I think

he's worried about what happened the other day."

"He should be. I almost called in a complaint myself."

"Me, too. Listen, I don't know where this thing is going so don't go running your mouth. I hardly know the girl."

"I can tell you're into her. Give it a shot," Travis suggested. "Ask her out again."

"I'm considering it."

They reached the fire truck and started unloading their groceries. On the way back to the station a call came in—par for the course. Groceries and Mila Barnes forgotten, they headed off to the scene.

10

The debacle with her vehicle set Mila back another hour. Fortunately for her, Carter Brubaker and Finley Jones were coming on shift and offered to give her a lift to an auto parts store, where she purchased a new battery. Carter was kind enough to install it for her.

By the time she got home, she was beat. She literally fell into bed, pulled the covers up over her head and didn't wake up until six in the evening.

Getting up was a chore. She was dreading another shift with Ledbetter.

Fortunately the next two shifts went by without incident. His attitude was still rotten and hers was headed in the same direction but they tolerated each other.

Just before her final shift of the week on Friday, Sammy Haynes approached her in the locker room. She was surprised to see him so late at night. He typically worked the day shift.

Sammy was an attractive guy with brown hair and striking green eyes. He was dressed for work, his gun and badge clipped to the waist of his dark colored trousers. When she'd first met him, she'd immediately liked his easy going, yet very professional work ethic. If only Ledbetter had an ounce of it…

"You got a minute?" he asked, leaning against the lockers. He had a file folder in his hands.

"Sure. What's up?"

"You went on a call the other day." He glanced at the file folder. "The name Kendall ring a bell?"

The memory of her altercation with Michael Kendall made her wince. "I remember."

"Can you run me through what happened?"

A little confused, she shrugged her shoulders. "It was a domestic dispute. Wife was inside the house and he wouldn't let her out. I insisted on speaking with her and he got upset. Why?" The idea that the incident was coming back to haunt her didn't sit well. She was beginning to wish she'd thrown Ledbetter under the bus for his behavior.

"He's dead."

She stared at him dumbly. "Who?"

"Michael Kendall. We found his body this morning in the house they shared—the same house you visited the other day."

She muttered an oath and reached up to rub at the tense muscles on the back of her neck. "The wife?"

"Nowhere to be found."

She hadn't been expecting the reply. "I thought you were going to tell me she was dead, too."

He shook his head. "We're still talking to neighbors. According to the woman next door, who appears to be quite the authority on their daily activities, they've been arguing off and on since he was released from jail Monday afternoon. She got suspicious and went to check on the wife when she didn't see any activity for a day or so. That's when she saw the husband lying in a pool of blood through the window."

Mila didn't want to picture anyone, Michael Kendall included, in such a position. She swallowed hard. "So did he kill himself?"

"Not unless he was able to shoot himself three times in the head."

The picture wasn't a pretty one. Even though she hadn't liked the abusive sonofabitch… "How did nobody hear a thing like that?"

"The woman next door has been in and out over the past couple of nights. Chances are, it happened while she was gone. Nobody else heard a thing."

The obvious suspect was the wife. She thought about the battered woman with the pathetic excuses for her husband's bad behavior. "Do you think the wife did it?"

"She would be the obvious suspect," he responded, confirming her hunch. "We're working through the evidence. I just figured I'd see what you thought."

"Have you spoken to Ledbetter?"

He grimaced and she realized right away that he was no fonder of her partner than she was.

"No. I read what he put in his report. From what I heard from Liam Colson, the report was bullshit." He arched a brow. "Care to explain that?"

"Not really." The reply was automatic.

He just stood there waiting patiently.

"We don't get along. It happens. I can handle Ledbetter."

"Can you?"

"I don't want you getting involved in this, Sammy. It will only make things worse."

"You have a right to tell your side of the story. If he's not doing his job, he shouldn't have it. He needs to have your back. This isn't a pissing contest."

"I can handle him," she said again, and repeated the same thing to herself inside her head.

"Okay," he relented, straightening. "If you say so. But I don't want to see you walk because of another guy like Jeff Winters. There's at least one in every department, Mila. Sooner or later, you're going to have to stand your ground and realize you're worth more if you want to stay in this profession."

"I've only been here two weeks," she said quietly.

"I realize that. But a problem is a problem. Any department that's worth a damn is going to back you up. I know Tennant. And I know of Ledbetter. You're not the first person to have a issue with him. The only reason he's still around is because of who his granddaddy is and the fact that we're short-handed as hell." He gave her arm a squeeze. "Let me know if you think of anything else about the other day that might help us with the Kendall case."

When he was gone, she expelled a breath and slammed her locker. Another great start to another long shift.

Knowing she had no choice, she went in search of Ledbetter.

. . .

Friday came along before Liam knew it. He was due to pick up Shaylee from school at three-thirty. She'd survived her first week as a first grader. And truth be told, she'd adjusted to her new teacher just fine. Mrs. Johnson was twenty-five, soft spoken and great with kids. He'd met her on Back-to School night, a couple of nights earlier.

Driving up in front of the Victorian after his shift, he noted Mila's SUV parked in its spot nearby. He hadn't heard anything from her all week. They'd both been busy. She'd been working and besides Shaylee's school commitments, he'd spent some time with his family—specifically with his mother and her new boyfriend.

David Wallace had turned out to be a nice surprise. While he was younger than what any of Debbie Colson's kids would have preferred, he was well-rounded, respectful and friendly. He appeared to dote on their mother, which made her smile. And that made Liam smile. Drew was on the same page as he was. Slade was slowly coming around. Jacy was a tough nut to crack. That was going to take a while.

Climbing from his vehicle, Liam strode up the walk to his apartment, stopping first at the mailbox and grabbing yesterday's mail. Bills,

bills and more bills. Swearing, he turned toward his porch. He was surprised to see Mila standing there, a bag in her hand. "Good morning. Bad time?"

He considered her. She was still wearing her uniform, which told him she'd probably just come in herself after an all-nighter. "What's in the bag?"

"Donuts and coffee. I figure I owe you."

He stepped around her to unlock the door. "I told you I don't keep track of debts. But come in anyway. I'm starving."

"You sure you're not too tired? I know you've been at work."

He waited just inside the door, already shrugging his jacket off. "So have you. Come on in."

She stepped into the apartment and he held his hand out for her jacket.

She slid it off and handed it over. "Calm night?"

"Not too bad. You?"

"You don't want to know."

He gestured to a chair at the breakfast bar. "That doesn't sound good."

She went to work unloading the donuts and coffee. "Do you remember Michael Kendall? The domestic abuser from last week?"

"How could I forget?" He took the cup of

coffee she offered even though he knew he should probably skip the caffeine. If he wanted to get a few hours of sleep before picking up Shaylee, the jolt wouldn't help.

"He's dead."

He stopped in mid-sip. "What?"

"He's dead." She took a large gulp of her own drink. "Sammy said they found his body yesterday morning. Apparently he was shot in the head three times."

He leaned against the breakfast bar. "That's awful. Did the wife do it?"

"They think so. She's missing."

"Wow. I don't know why I'm surprised."

"I'm a little surprised myself. Not because one of them is dead, but because of *which* one of them is dead. I would have put money on *him* killing *her*."

He thought about that. "Maybe he tried. Maybe that's why he's dead now."

"Maybe." She sat down on a stool. "I hate outcomes like this. I wish I could have done something more for her. I knew they were on a very slippery slope."

He sat down next to her. "It's not your fault. You did your job. She didn't want your help."

She shrugged and nodded, taking a bite of powdered donut. "It still bothers me."

"She chose to turn the other cheek. Bottom

line is he shouldn't have gotten out of jail. He assaulted you. What the hell happened?"

"I didn't look at the papers but I'm assuming he posted bail." She wiped her mouth with a napkin. "Anyway, it's made for an interesting day. The investigation is ongoing. I just wonder where she is."

"If she's responsible for his death, she'd better be long gone by now—like in Mexico or something." He took a bite of his own donut. "Change in subject but I've been meaning to text you. Did you get your car fixed?"

"Battery was dead Monday morning when I went to head home. Carter Brubaker helped me get a new one and put it in. It's good as new."

"I'm sorry. If I could have helped you out more I would have."

She shook her head. "You helped me out enough. I was only a few minutes late to work. Unfortunately I bumped into Tennant on my way into the building."

He winced. "That sucks."

"Yeah, what are the chances of him being there at midnight?" She finished off her donut. "I didn't get into trouble or anything so all is good."

He found himself staring at a smear of powdered sugar that was caked in a corner of her mouth.

"What?" she asked, licking her lips.

The motion was hot enough to make him swallow hard, despite its innocent intent.

"Okay, I know I'm a pig with donuts but…" Her words trailed off when he reached forward and brushed at the crumbs with his forefinger. Their eyes locked.

Suddenly the air in the room seemed to dissipate. Before he knew what he was doing, he was kissing her.

She opened immediately, their tongues sliding together in an erotic dance.

Donuts and coffee forgotten, he tangled his fingers in her hair and pulled her closer, into the cradle of his thighs.

The kissing went on for a few minutes. His lips slid down the side of her jaw, reminding him of the bruise she'd had there. When he took a minute to examine it, he noticed it was pretty much healed.

Their noses bumped and their eyes met.

"You taste like donuts." Her mouth broke into a smile. "I really like donuts."

He found himself grinning, too. "Yeah, me, too." Their mouths met again, this time more urgently. For the first time in a long time, he found himself wanting a woman. He cupped her hips with his hands and pulled her closer, grinding their mid-sections together.

"I should probably go home and let you get some sleep," she said against his mouth.

He realized pretty quickly that he didn't want her to. "Or you could stay."

Breathlessly, she looked into his eyes. "Is that what you really want?"

"Oh yeah." He didn't hesitate. "But I should be honest with you. I'm not sure where I'm at beyond wanting you like hell. I'm still figuring my life out."

"So am I." She lifted her head. "It's been a while for me. I don't do things like this all the time. I know I've come across as pretty forward but—"

"You don't owe me any explanations."

She took his hands and entwined their fingers. "So I'll ask you again. Do you want me to go?"

"No." He stood, backing up toward the hallway. She followed without much persuasion. Once they were inside his bedroom, he nudged her toward the bed until the backs of her knees hit and she landed on her butt on the mattress.

A yowl sounded from behind her and he realized the damn cat was perched on his pillow.

"You must be Lucky," she crooned, turning and giving the cat a pat on the head. Surprisingly, the beast didn't hiss. He trotted closer to Mila and rubbed his head against her arm.

Liam took the opportunity and picked the cat up before he could get too comfortable. "Later, bud."

Lucky hissed again as he was set out in the hallway. The door was promptly shut in his face.

"That was mean," Mila admonished, but she was smiling.

"You want him in here with us? His claws are like razor blades." He bent, caging her in with his arms as she shook her head. Their foreheads touched and their eyes met. He came over her, carefully bracing his weight on his hands. Their mouths immediately crushed together, tongues tangling.

She dragged the tails of his work shirt free from his pants, her fingers sliding up his back.

He reached for the buttons on her top, undoing them one at a time. "There's something kind of sexy about a woman in uniform." He leaned over and slid his tongue along her newly exposed collar bone and up the side of her neck, eliciting a breathy moan from deep in her throat.

"Maybe you'll find me sexier out of it," she suggested pointedly.

He chuckled, lifting her tank top and exposing her lacy, white bra. "I have no doubt."

He moved a cup aside and covered one taut nipple with his mouth.

Her head fell back and she shut her eyes in ecstasy.

He repeated his ministrations on the other breast.

Before long, she was writhing beneath him. She grappled for his belt buckle, dragging at the metal and trying to pry it loose.

He lifted, giving her better access.

When she had his pants open, her fingers wrapped around him and he just about lost it right there. It had been too long for him — too long since he'd had a woman's hands on him.

He let her have her way with him until he couldn't stand it anymore. Then he went for her cargos, making quick work of pulling them, and the panties underneath, down her legs. She kicked them to the floor while he got rid of his own. When the last of their clothing was gone, she scooted up toward the headboard, her head resting against one of his pillows. He followed, reaching into the nightstand for a condom.

They came together quickly once he was sheathed. He moaned against her mouth and began to move.

She wrapped her legs around him and met him thrust for thrust.

They moved in unison, racing toward the

same peak. He used his fingers on her and pushed her over the edge, knowing he wasn't going to last long.

She groaned against his mouth and he stilled inside her and came apart himself.

As the spasms faded, he braced himself and lifted his head. She was smiling and he found himself smiling, too. "You're right, I think you're sexier out of your uniform."

She started to laugh as he disengaged himself and rolled onto his back.

Snuggling against him, she rested her chin against his chest, meeting his gaze. "This day didn't start out so great but it's looking up."

He accepted the kiss she offered, his tongue making quick work of sliding between her teeth and doing a thorough exploration of her mouth.

"I know you get Shaylee back today. What time do you have to pick her up?" she asked when the kiss finally ended.

"Not until three-thirty so don't get any ideas. I'm not done with you yet." He brushed some auburn hair back from her face. "Unless you have other plans."

"I might be persuaded to stay." She pulled at the covers until they were snuggled together underneath them. "Maybe we could take a little rest and pick this up after we've regained our energy."

"I like the way you think." He allowed his eyes to drop closed, content to hold her as he fell asleep.

When he awoke, it was to the sound of his phone ringing. It was somewhere across the room where they'd tossed his pants earlier.

Cursing, he glanced at the bedside clock. It was nearly one. They'd been asleep for four hours. Mila was still snuggled against him so he carefully set her aside.

Locating his pants, he dug through the pockets until he found his cell. Peering at the caller ID, he grimaced. Shelby was calling. He silenced the call and glanced behind him where Mila was just starting to stir. She stretched her arms out above her head and smiled sleepily. "Hey."

Her smile was contagious. "Hey. I think we slept a little longer than we planned."

She followed his gaze to the clock. "Shoot. I'm sorry, I totally dozed off." She started to get up.

"There's no rush. I need to return this call though. I'll be right back."

He snatched his pants and pulled them on before heading into the other room and calling Shelby back.

"Sorry to bother you," she greeted. "I know you're supposed to pick Shaylee up from school today but she's home. The school nurse called. She's got a fever so Pam picked her up early and brought her home."

Immediately annoyed, he pinched the bridge of his nose. "Why didn't you call me? I would have picked her up."

"I figured you were sleeping, Liam. I know you worked all night."

"It's my week, Shelby. Sick or not, I'm picking her up."

"I never said you couldn't." Shelby's voice immediately turned angry. "You don't have to talk to me like you think I'm trying to pull one over on you. But you should know she doesn't feel well. She's upstairs sleeping. If you want to come and get her, that's up to you."

He sighed in frustration and told himself not to overreact. The bottom line was that Shaylee was sick. It wasn't about him and it wasn't about Shelby. "Is there anything she needs?"

"No. I'm sure she'll feel better in a day or two. Like I said, if you want me to wake her, I will. Or you can see how she's feeling tomorrow."

He knew the right thing to do was let Shaylee be. If she wasn't feeling good, she wouldn't want to uproot and move to his place. Still…

"This isn't my fault, Liam. I'm just the messenger."

"I realize that. Have her call me when she

wakes up and we'll decide what she wants to do."

"Okay." She hung up.

Cursing, he shoved the phone back into his pocket.

"Everything okay?"

He turned at the sound of Mila's voice. She was standing in the hallway fully dressed, her shoes in her hands. "Everything is fine. Shaylee's not feeling good. She went home early from school."

"Oh no. I'm sorry."

"I'm sure it's just a bug. The minute school starts..." His voice trailed off and he watched as she sat down and shoved her feet into her sneakers. "You don't have to leave. She's sleeping right now so I'm going to see how she's doing when she wakes up."

"I should go anyway." She finished tying her shoes and stood up again. "I'm sure you have stuff to do."

He folded his arms over his bare chest. "Not really." He wasn't sure what had happened to sour her mood between the time he'd left her in his bed and now. A span of five minutes had passed.

"I didn't intend to stay this long. She gave him an awkward smile. "Thanks though. For the food. For the..." She shrugged. "Just thanks."

He arched a brow as he watched her head for the door like fire was licking at her heels. "You're welcome."

For a good minute after she'd gone, he stared at the closed front door. He was truly perplexed. *Women.* Who the hell could figure them out?

11

When Mila was behind her apartment door, she sighed in relief. She wasn't sure exactly what had happened downstairs. One minute she'd been content lying in Liam's bed, relishing in the scent of him on the pillows beneath her head. The next, she'd heard his end of his conversation with his ex-wife and started to sweat.

The realization that he had a child hit her straight away. He was fully responsible for a little girl. A little girl who idolized him. Why had that fact not fully hit her before? She'd met the kid!

Chastising herself for being so clueless, she raked a hand through her hair. Her phone began to ring and she tensed when her brother's number popped up. Reid had terrible timing.

Knowing better than to ignore him, she answered the call curtly.

"What's wrong?" he asked in greeting.

"What do you mean what's wrong? You're the one who called me." She went across the room to the kitchen and got the coffee pot going.

"I called you because I wanted to see how things are going. I can tell by your voice that something's wrong."

"All I said to you was hello."

"It's your tone."

She bit back a curse. "Nothing's wrong, Reid. I just got in the door. I've got groceries in my arms." The lie spilled off her tongue uneasily.

"Again? You just shopped last weekend."

She shut her eyes and counted to ten inside her head, willing her wits to gather. Her brother knew her far too well. "Is there a law against shopping more than once a week?"

"No. I've been saying that very thing to you for years."

She poured herself some coffee. "How are you Reid?" She decided to turn the tables on him. She really didn't want him to ask about her. She had no good news for him.

"I'm good, Mila. I'm calling to see how things are with you. How's work?"

So much for her distraction attempt. "Good," she lied. "I'm settling in."

There was a space of silence. "You're a terrible liar. What's really going on?"

Frustrated, she set her coffee cup down. "I'm working at fitting in. It's a process."

"Fair enough," he shocked her by relenting. "So tell me about your neighbor downstairs."

She choked on a swallow of coffee and had to clear her throat several times. She'd almost forgotten Reid had met Liam the previous weekend.

He didn't wait for her response. "That says a lot."

"I'm choking to death," she finally managed to get out.

"Yeah, I hear you. I also saw the way you looked at him last weekend. I saw the way he looked at me."

"At *you*?"

"He thought I was competition at first."

She hadn't noticed that at all. "That's ridiculous."

"Guys know this stuff, sis. Trust me."

Leaning a hip against the counter, she thought about that.

"Don't scramble to come up with more lies. Just tell me about him."

"There's nothing to tell." Another lie. They

were stacking up nicely.

"He's a firefighter. That's not a bad profession. It's gainful employment with a good pension."

He was so matter of fact she found herself rolling her eyes. "So what?"

"So he's not a deadbeat. Why are you being so evasive about him? Clearly you like him. I think it's great."

"You do?"

"Sure. I'd like to see you settle down. I wouldn't worry so much about you if you would."

"Good grief, that's a bit premature. I don't know him very well."

"So what are your intentions?"

"You sound like someone's father."

"Just answer the question. You'll get me off the phone much quicker if you do."

Sighing, she sat down on the couch and thought it over. After her reaction earlier…

"Has he asked you out?"

Realizing if she wanted an honest opinion she needed to come clean, she flopped back against the cushions. "I asked him out. He took me to a movie and dinner. We had a good time. I didn't see him for a week. Then this morning, I brought him breakfast." She paused. "And slept with him."

He muttered an oath. "That's more information than I was after."

"You asked."

She heard him blow out a breath. "Okay, so why do you sound so frazzled?"

"Because he has a kid. A six-year-old."

"No kidding? Girl or boy?"

"A girl."

"Huh. Okay, well is that such a big deal?"

"Kind of. It's a small person that he's responsible for. I don't know how serious I'm ready to be. I don't imagine it's in her best interest for me to keep fooling around with him."

"A lot of people have kids and go on to date after a divorce. I should ask though, what happened? Why's he divorced?"

"The wife cheated. With a woman. She's engaged to the woman currently and living with her."

"Shit. That sucks."

"Yeah."

"Well, you've already slept with him. You're already involved more than is appropriate if you're planning to bail."

"Thanks for that."

"You want me to bullshit?"

A part of her did. Just once, she'd like someone to tell her what she *wanted* to hear.

"Bullshit isn't going to help you," he said

unapologetically. "He seems like a nice guy. Why not see what happens?"

"All of my previous relationships have been trainwrecks."

"Your point?"

"I don't want another trainwreck. I was just planning on having fun."

"So have fun then."

"You're not helping."

"What do you want me to say, Mila?"

What *did* she want him to say? Leaning forward again, she stared at the carpet. "I think the timing's off. For him and for me. He's still piecing his life back together. I've got a lot going on, too." She repeated that inside her head several times.

"I guess that's your answer then."

"Yeah," she agreed. "I guess."

"Listen, I need to get going. I've got to head up to the mountain. Don't stress things so much. And don't sleep with him again until you decide what you want. Sex muddles up everything."

It was true. She agreed and hung up. She had the sudden urge to apologize to Liam for her odd departure. She'd read the confusion in his expression when she'd left that morning. She'd jumped into things with both feet, then backed away just as abruptly. Usually she was far more sensible than this. What had gotten into her?

. . .

Liam called Shelby again around four o'clock. He'd spoken to Shaylee himself. She was awake but still didn't feel great so they agreed he would check back in the morning.

After that, he peered into his fridge in search of something for dinner. Pulling out a loaf of cheese and some deli meat, he prepared to make a sandwich. Before he got the chance, there was a knock on his door.

He crossed the room and opened it. He frowned at the sight of Mila standing there, a sheepish look on her face. After the way she'd left earlier, he hadn't expected to see her again — at least not for a while.

"Don't slam the door in my face. I'm here to apologize."

He didn't readily invite her in. Instead, he leaned against the doorjamb. "Don't apologize on my account. You don't owe me anything."

"You have a daughter."

He narrowed his eyes. "Yes, I know."

She sighed deeply. "We slept together."

"Is this a riddle?"

"I've never slept with a man that has children."

"You knew about Shaylee before we slept

together." He was completely confused at this point.

"I know I did. I guess I didn't think things through."

A little frustrated, he shook his head at her. "Why are you here, Mila? I don't expect anything from you. I'm not usually the one-night-stand type but I'll make an exception in this case." He started to shut the door.

"Wait!"

Sighing, he met her gaze again. "You're right, I have a daughter. She comes before anyone else in my life. She's six years old. I can't argue with that. And I can't change it."

She scrubbed a hand over her face. "I know."

When she didn't say anything more, he leaned against the doorjamb again. "So why are you still standing here?"

"I'm not sure." She shoved her hands into the pockets of her jeans. "I've been trying to talk myself out of liking you all day. Obviously I've failed."

"It's not so obvious to me," he replied dryly. "You're sending me mixed signal after mixed signal."

"I'm sorry," she repeated.

"Stop apologizing." He turned and walked away from the door. "If you want to keep talking, come inside."

"What about Shaylee?"

"She's staying with her mom tonight. She's still not feeling well." He reached the counter and went back to work making his sandwich while she stepped into the apartment and shut the door. Without asking, he made one for her. When he was done, he slid it across to her and grabbed some water for them both. Then he met her gaze. "Do you have a problem with kids or something?"

"Of course not. I like kids."

"Then what's your big concern with my daughter? You've met her. She's not typically a brat. She's a good kid."

She stared at him for a long moment. "I know that. I like her."

"Okay. Then what's all this about?"

She hesitated. Eventually she sighed. "I guess I heard you talking to your ex on the phone this morning and I got scared."

"Scared of what?"

"Hurting her. Letting her down. I like you a lot—more than I want to. The minute I met her, I liked her, too. But I'm not ready for any kind of committed relationship. Not with anyone. I may never be."

He thought about that. Leaning over, he rested his arms on the counter. "I may not either, Mila. I haven't even dated that much since my divorce. I'm perfectly happy being single. We can still see each other. It's not like we're going to be living together. We're figuring each other out right now. The only thing I ask of you is that if you decide you're done with me, don't just dump on Shaylee. She's big on friendship. I was a little worried about that when Drew started seeing Amber."

"I wouldn't do that."

He straightened and shrugged his shoulders. "Then we're good. Let's just take things one day at a time."

She eyed the sandwich in front of her. "You keep plying me with food."

"You keep showing up at mealtime."

She grinned and took a seat at the counter.

12

Mila stayed the night with Liam. The more time they spent together, the more she found herself liking him. He was funny and smart and pretty easy going. They watched a couple of movies together—action flicks this time. They shared some ice cream. Then they shared his bed. The sex was phenomenal. They were more than compatible in every way.

The next morning, she knew she had things to do and he needed to deal with his daughter. They said their goodbyes and she went back to her apartment. When she reached her door, she was surprised to find a notecard taped to it. Curiously, she snatched the card and went inside. Opening the flaps, she read the message written there.

Meet me today at noon. Fred Griffin Park. Down by the water.

That was it. No name signed, nothing.

She read the note again, perplexed. The handwriting was neat cursive. She immediately found herself thinking it had been written by a woman. Typically, men scrawled things rather than writing so perfectly.

Tossing the cryptic notecard down, she ran over the possible authors in her head. At first, nobody came to mind. She was new in town. She really had no friends to speak of. She was just getting to know her co-workers—Ledbetter aside. None of them would leave such a mysterious request for her.

So who had?

All at once, an idea occurred to her. She thought about the young girl she'd met the previous week. The one from the burglary.

Jana Whitfield.

The note had to be from her. There was no other logical explanation.

She contemplated her options. Proper protocol would be to notify her partner of her suspicions, and then their superior.

She nixed that idea immediately. There was no way in hell she was involving Ledbetter. He'd screwed up the investigation to begin with.

Setting some coffee to percolate, she stared at the notecard. She had no concrete proof that it was the Whitfield girl who'd left the request. Until she knew what she was dealing with, she was going to have to decide what to do on her own.

She poured some coffee and glanced at her watch. It was just after ten. Fred Griffin Park was about ten miles from her apartment. It was in a less than desirable part of town, not far from the river.

She sat at the kitchen table and contemplated the situation. She could ignore the note. It was quite possibly just a hoax—a prank. Some people had a very odd sense of humor.

Her instincts immediately told her that wasn't the case here.

The only other option she had was to do as the person asked and go to the park.

Leaving her coffee, she went to the bathroom and showered. After dressing, she checked her service revolver and made sure it was ready to go if she needed it. Then she attached it to a holster hidden underneath her jacket.

Grabbing her phone and her car keys, she headed for her SUV.

The late September air was cold and crisp. There was a light rain falling so she turned on her windshield wipers as soon as she had the car started.

The drive took about twenty minutes. There was more traffic than she expected. She reached the park just before noon. The place was pretty much deserted because of the weather.

Re-checking for her weapon, she climbed from her vehicle and glanced around.

Fred Griffin Park wasn't really set up for kids. It was more of a jogging park — a place for picnics or bike riding. There was a trail off to the left that she figured out pretty quickly led down to the river.

Taking a deep breath, she headed that way. The hike took her about ten minutes. When she hit the clearing and saw the water, she wasn't sure where to go.

"I wasn't sure you'd come."

The voice was so startling, it caused her to jump and reach for her weapon automatically. She hadn't sensed anyone's presence.

Turning, she saw the outline of a small person step from the shadows of the trees. It was definitely a woman, judging by the sound of her voice. She was wearing jeans and an over-sized, dark blue sweatshirt. A hood was pulled down low on her head until she lifted it back. Mila got another shock as she realized the woman was not Jana Whitfield.

"I'm unarmed. You don't need your gun."

Her fingers still clasping her weapon, Mila backed up a little, her eyes carefully perusing the area around the woman she now recognized as Vanessa Kendall.

Michael Kendall's wife.

The woman currently wanted for his murder.

"Please hear me out before you call for the police."

"I *am* the police," Mila said quietly.

"I just want to talk. Please." Vanessa sidestepped and walked toward the water, her hands in the air. "See? I have no weapons."

Mila still kept her guard up. "You left that note on my door. Why?"

"I told you; I want to talk."

"You're wanted for murder, Mrs. Kendall. You need to turn yourself into the police."

"I can't do that."

"You have to. Even if you get away now, it's only a matter of time before the police hunt you down."

"You don't understand. If you'll just listen, I'll explain everything to you." Vanessa Kendall's eyes were moist suddenly. She exhaled deeply. "Please just give me a chance. I wouldn't have come to you if I wasn't desperate. I've got no place else to go."

Mila felt pity for the woman. She'd clearly been through hell with her husband. He'd been a bad man. Hell, Mila had experienced that firsthand. Still, that wasn't a license to kill. "I have to call for back up. And you need to stay right where you are with your hands where I can see them." Mila dug into her pocket for her phone, still keeping her weapon poised and ready.

"I didn't kill him."

Mila's fingers were fumbling with her phone. She stopped before she hit the button for 911. When she looked into Vanessa Kendall's eyes, the desperation was still there, but there was a flicker of something else, too. *Fear.* It had Mila halting in her tracks.

"Just please give me ten minutes. If after you hear what I have to say, you still want to call for help, I won't stop you."

Mila hesitated. She knew she was skating on very thin ice.

"Ten minutes," Vanessa repeated. "Please."

Knowing she was breaking all kinds of rules, Mila shoved her phone back into her pocket. "Ten minutes. And I want to check you over myself for weapons. Then we'll sit in my car."

Vanessa stepped forward and lifted her arms up so Mila could pat her down. Mila found no weapons on her.

They walked back up the trail to the parking lot. Once they were seated in Mila's SUV, the heat running, Mila gave the woman her full attention. "Ten minutes starts now."

"Michael was bad man, Officer Barnes. A terrible man. What you saw the other night? That was nothing. He's broken my arms, my collar bone. He's blackened my eyes more times than I can tell you. I've covered bruises for years. But I loved him." She rubbed at her arms where the rain had soaked her sweatshirt. "No matter how hard I tried to hate him, I couldn't. Even when he cheated on me." She shook her head. "I know I sound pathetic. Don't look at me that way."

"You could have left him. You didn't have to kill him."

"I already told you I didn't."

Mila was still skeptical. "He beat you and was arrested. You refused to press charges against him. When he was charged with assaulting an officer, you provided bail. You should have just left him in jail."

"That's just it, I did."

"Someone got him out."

"It wasn't me."

Nothing made any sense. Mila hadn't checked the reports or the paperwork after Michael Kendall had been released. All she knew for sure was that someone had bailed him out and the cost had been high.

"You saw where I live, Officer. I don't have the kind of money it would have taken to get him out of jail. I can't lie and say I wasn't working on it, but I hit a wall. He found bail somewhere else."

"If that's true, I'll be able to prove it."

"I'm counting on that. That's why I left you that note."

"Just because you didn't bail him out of jail doesn't mean you didn't kill him."

Sighing, Vanessa scrubbed her hands over her face. "I know what this all looks like. But it's not what it seems. I wasn't there the night he died. We'd been fighting. He was pounding on me again, threatening to kill me this time. And I knew he meant it. After the trip to jail…" She shook her head, a trail of tears running down her cheeks. "He was the worst I'd ever seen him. I knew I had to get out."

Mila told herself not to get sucked into the tale. People were liars, especially when they were drowning in circumstances like Vanessa Kendall's. That being said, her story, crazy as it seemed, was credible.

"My neighbor—Mrs. Crawford," Vanessa went on. "She saw me leave on Tuesday night. It was late and Michael had fallen asleep on the couch, drunk as a skunk. That was the last time I saw him. It was the last time I was home. He was alive when I left. I swear it."

"Did you speak with Mrs. Crawford?"

Vanessa bit her bottom lip. "No. She was always getting into our business. I had bruises and I didn't want her to make another big commotion and call the police again so I just took off. But I know she saw me."

"Even if she did, there's nothing saying you didn't come back and kill your husband."

Frustrated, Vanessa swore.

"If you could prove any of this, it would be one thing—" Mila began.

"Ask Mrs. Crawford for access to her security cameras. She's got two in the back of her house and one in the front. Maybe one of them shows me leaving."

Or shows you coming back, Mila thought to herself.

"I'm telling you the truth. Do you really think I would ask you for help if I was guilty? I'd be in Mexico right now if that were the case." Vanessa shook her head. "I didn't even know Michael was dead until I heard about the shooting on the news two days ago. I've been frantic ever since."

Mila thought her options over. She knew what she should do is call for back up. The best thing for Vanessa at this point was for her to turn herself in and let Sammy and Slade sort the mess out.

"If you check out what I've told you, I'm telling you you'll see it's all true."

Mila pulled out her phone, knowing what she had to do. "I will make sure your story gets checked out. If it's true, the detectives on the case will be able to help you. They're your best hope."

Before Mila could so much as push the button to lock the car doors, Vanessa was out of the vehicle and running.

Cursing, Mila followed, her weapon in hand.

With the rain coming down in sheets, it was slippery as hell. Twice, she lost her footing and nearly hit the ground. Once they were on the trail, she realized she was at a definite disadvantage. She had sneakers on and they were no match for the rough terrain. About halfway in, she turned her ankle and fell hard. She forced herself back to her feet but when she looked up, she didn't see Vanessa Kendall anywhere. It was as if the woman had vanished into thin air.

13

Mila knew she was in trouble by the look on Sammy's face when he walked into the interrogation room at the precinct, Slade Colson on his heels.

The two men were dressed in plain clothes — jeans and PPB T-shirts. They had their badges and guns, but it was clear they'd been called in on their own time to deal with the latest developments in the Kendall case.

Sammy sat down first, dropping his folded hands on the table.

Slade sat nearby, letting out a weary sigh.

"What the hell are you doing, Barnes?" This came from Sammy.

She was expecting the question. She'd been

going over her answer for the past thirty minutes while she'd waited for the detectives to show up. Sadly, she hadn't come up with a great response. Nothing that would explain how she'd had Vanessa Kendall—a wanted woman suspected of murder, no less—in her grasp and let her go.

"I want you to start your story at the beginning. How did Vanessa Kendall manage to contact you?" Slade asked, taking the floor.

Mila shifted uncomfortably. "She left a note on my door."

"A note," Sammy repeated. He arched a brow. "So you're telling me she left a note on your door, you read it, and then decided it was a good idea for you to run off and meet her by yourself—even though you were well aware that she's wanted for murder." He wasn't questioning her, more like stating the facts.

"I didn't know it was her. When I first saw the note, I thought she was Jana Whitfield."

Sammy gave her a confused stare. "Who's Jana Whitfield?"

"She's the teenager who was involved in a B&E Ledbetter and I responded to the other night."

Both Slade and Sammy continued to stare at her, perplexed.

"It's a long story," she stammered, hating the scrutinizing looks in their eyes. They'd both been supportive in helping her get on with the PPB—two of her biggest allies. Seeing skepticism in their eyes was a tough pill to swallow.

"Shorten it," Slade ordered, clearly growing impatient.

She hesitated.

"Is this more of the crap you've got going on with Ledbetter?" Sammy asked, tapping his fingers against the table irritably. "Because I warned you about that. I told you to nip it in the bud."

Sighing, she rubbed at her throbbing temples. "Ledbetter and I responded to a B&E last week. I knew something was off about the teenager who witnessed the crime. I had a bad feeling something more had happened to her, besides the burglary."

"So you're saying you suspected sexual assault," Slade figured out pretty quickly.

She shrugged and nodded. "Ledbetter took the situation over before I could question the girl myself. By the time I got to her, she was wrapped up tight as a drum. She wasn't admitting anything, but I knew..." She leaned back in her chair. "I left her my card, hoping maybe when she calmed down, she'd want to talk. That's why I thought the note on my door was from her. I thought maybe she'd tracked me down. If I'd suspected it was Vanessa Kendall…" The rest of her sentence went unsaid.

Slade swore.

"Once you figured out it was her, you still didn't call for back up. Why?" Sammy asked.

She bit her bottom lip. No matter how she put things, she was digging herself a hole. Sighing, she gave up on sugar coating her explanation. "She told me she's innocent. I was interested in hearing her side of the story."

"Are you shitting me?" Slade asked.

She just remained silent, knowing she'd said enough.

Sammy blew out a breath. "We've got a serious problem here now. When Tennant gets a load of this…" He shook his head. "You're smarter than this, Barnes."

She knew he was right. "I can't turn back time." She thought about her conversation with Vanessa Kendall. "While I know I've screwed up, I had a pretty lengthy conversation with Vanessa Kendall. Maybe if I share what she told me it will help with your investigation."

"What would have helped our investigation is if you'd freaking called us when you had her in your car." Slade scowled at her.

For a moment, he reminded her so much of Liam she had to blink twice to convince herself he wasn't his brother. "She says she's innocent," she finally said, for lack of anything better.

"Most murderers do," Slade countered.

"She has a pretty credible story, Slade. If you'll listen, I'll tell you what she told me."

Slade exchanged a glance with Sammy.

Sammy leaned against the back of his chair. "Go ahead. We'll listen."

"She says she left the Kendall house Tuesday night. Do you have a time of death yet?"

"We do."

He made no move to fill her in on the details and she ignored the pang of irritation she felt suddenly at being left out of the loop. "I know his body wasn't found until Thursday morning, right?"

Sammy nodded.

"She swears he was alive when she left. They'd been arguing. He was upset about the fact that he'd spent the weekend in jail. He'd been beating on her since coming home. He threatened to kill her this time."

"*This time*? What makes you think this was the first time?" Slade asked.

"I'm using her words, Slade. She said *this time*, as though he hadn't done so before." She looked Sammy in the eye. "She was scared. He got drunk and passed out and she left. I don't know exactly what time, but she said it was late.

She swears her neighbor saw her leave. Have you looked at any surveillance footage? Security cameras in the area?"

"We're working on that," Sammy assured her. "Most of the neighbors don't have that type of surveillance and the ones who do have their cameras pointed at their own property."

"Mrs. Crawford. That's the woman Vanessa mentioned you should check with."

"The older lady next door," Slade clarified. "Widow, late fifties. The neighborhood Nosy Nellie. I spoke to her myself. She's the one who called in the body."

"Did she offer you surveillance?"

"She showed me some footage. The camera angles weren't beneficial to our investigation. They're mainly pointed at her backyard and the driveway in front of her house. She didn't mention anything about Vanessa Kendall leaving the house Tuesday night."

"Shit." Mila had been hoping for some type of smoking gun here. A thought occurred to her. "Who bailed him out?"

"Of jail?" Sammy shrugged. "Far as I know, the wife."

"She says she didn't."

"While I realize she seems to have done quite a job on you, Barnes, don't you think it's possible that she's lying?" Slade asked.

"Of course I do. But don't you think it's a good idea to check?"

"We'll check," Sammy assured her. "Did she say anything else?"

"Not really. She loved him. He put her through hell but she loved him."

"That doesn't mean she didn't kill him."

He was right, so Mila didn't argue.

"I can't cover for you here," Sammy warned her. "I'll do my best to explain things to Tennant the same way you've explained them to us, but you're probably in for an ass-chewing."

She'd already figured as much. She gathered her purse and left the precinct.

The drive home was somber. She was pretty convinced she'd just sealed her fate with the PPB—maybe with law enforcement entirely. The possibility was daunting.

She went straight up to her apartment and hibernated inside. She'd dropped Liam a text earlier and checked on Shaylee. According to him, she was fine. He'd picked her up that afternoon and she was lounging on his couch, watching cartoons.

Changing into some pajamas, she curled up on her own couch and stared at the television, not bothering to turn it on.

How in the hell had her life become such a mess in such a short amount of time? She'd been convinced getting away from Jeff Winters and his condescending, know-it-all attitude would fix everything for her professionally. At this point, he was starting to look like a saint.

An hour later, just as she was dozing off, she heard a knock on the door.

Sighing, she tossed her blanket aside and went to the peephole. Liam was on the stoop. Opening the door, she peered at him curiously.

"You okay?"

She gave him a questioning stare.

"I just got off the phone with Slade. He told me what happened."

A bit embarrassed, she folded her arms over her chest. "Did you tell him that we…?"

"Of course not. He mentioned you in a nonchalant manner. He's pretty ticked off."

"I know he is." She raked a hand through her hair. "Isn't Shaylee downstairs?"

"She's sleeping on the couch. I won't leave her for long. I just wanted to check in on you. Slade said he and Sammy were pretty hard on you."

"They were mild compared to what Tennant's going to do to me when he finds out what I did."

He leaned against the wall outside the door. "Maybe he'll just yell at you a little. I've met the guy. He's fair."

"I screwed up someone else's investigation,

Liam. I had a suspected murderer in my grasp and I let her get away."

"Not purposely."

"Nobody screws up on purpose. He won't care." She sighed heavily. "It doesn't matter. I'm starting to think this whole move to Portland was a big mistake. Ever since I got here, everything's gone downhill. I'm going to be standing in line for free cheese by Monday morning."

"That's a little dramatic. And it hasn't been *all* bad, right?"

The way he cocked his head to the side was endearing and she found her mood softening. "No. You're definitely the only light in a very dark tunnel."

He grinned and reached for her. She let him pull her against his chest, content to lose herself in his embrace. He felt good and he smelled good and for the moment, that was enough.

Hearing the sound of someone clearing their throat in the distance, they instantly separated. That's when Mila saw Slade standing at the bottom of the stairs, Sammy behind him. She abruptly stiffened. Her nightmare instantly intensified.

"I'll be down in a minute," Liam called to them.

"We're not here to see you," Slade replied

cautiously. "At least Sammy's not."

Liam turned back to her questioningly. "You want me to stay?"

"Go take care of Shaylee. I'll be fine."

He backed up hesitantly and hit the steps. Sammy crossed paths with him on his way up. Slade didn't follow. Mila didn't miss the look he sent his brother's way when they were eye to eye at the bottom of the stairs.

"You got a minute?" Sammy was right in front of her before she knew it.

"What about him?" She gestured to Slade, who it seemed was more interested in Liam than he was in her.

Sammy brushed him aside. "He's here to check on Shaylee. Can I come inside?"

She backed up and gestured for him to enter the apartment. "You want some coffee? That's about all I have on hand."

"I'm good. Can we sit?"

She nodded and led him to the couch, where they both sat down.

"So I looked in to what you said this afternoon. Don't get too excited but I was able to confirm that Vanessa Kendall wasn't lying to you about not bailing out her husband."

Mila's mood instantly perked up. "She wasn't?"

"No. A woman by the name of Taya Randall

posted the bail. She listed herself as a friend."

"A friend," Mila repeated.

"That's what she called herself on paper." He dangled his hands between his knees. "When we spoke with her face to face, she was apprehensive at first. Eventually she admitted she and Michael had a relationship."

"Vanessa told me her husband was cheating on her."

"Taya Randall says he was going to leave Vanessa—that the marriage was over. She knew nothing about his abusive nature."

"So she says. Like you said, people lie."

"Maybe." He straightened. "Everything she told us checks out. She admitted to the affair, admitted she bailed him out. There's no proof anywhere that she's lying about him leaving his wife."

"Vanessa didn't say anything to me about the marriage being over. She left Michael the other night because she was scared, not because she was getting a divorce."

"I know what she told you, Mila. I'm telling you there are two sides to every story."

"What makes you think Taya Randall didn't kill Michael Kendall?"

"Nothing. She's very clearly on my radar. But she's got a pretty good alibi. She works as a nurse at Portland General. She's been on the night shift off and on in the E.R. During the time period we've determined Kendall was murdered, she was on the clock."

"We both know alibis aren't air-tight sometimes. Especially an alibi like that. She could have snuck away. Maybe she was mad because he wasn't leaving his wife like he'd promised her. Maybe she found out he was lying about the relationship altogether. The scenarios are endless."

"We're looking into all that. It's going to take some time. I just wanted to let you know we followed up. I know you're upset. I don't blame you. But you've made some bad decisions here."

She knew he was right.

"I spoke to Tennant, too. I'm sure he's going to call you in but I managed to smooth things over somewhat. Now that we've got some information that panned out in the investigation, he's not as pissed as he would have been." He gave her a warning look. "I mentioned what happened with Ledbetter. I had no choice. Your partnership with him is interfering with the quality of work you two are doing. Something has to change."

"Great." She couldn't really be mad at him. She'd dug this hole for herself.

He stood. "I should get back to work. I'll keep you in the loop when I can."

"Thanks." She followed him to the door.

He turned at the last minute. "You're a good cop, Barnes. Don't throw in the towel just yet."

"What makes you think I plan to?"

"The look on your face today was less than encouraging. After what happened in Eugene…" He seemed sympathetic. "We've had this conversation before. Hold steady and keep your head up. Something tells me things will be okay if you do."

She nodded and watched him go, feeling significantly better than she'd felt a few hours earlier.

. . .

Before Liam even reached the door to his apartment, Slade's voice was in his ear. "I guess I should have seen this coming."

Liam turned, meeting his brother's gaze. "Probably. You're the one who encouraged me to give her a chance."

Slade leaned against the wall thoughtfully. "I suppose I was."

"So why do you look so distressed now?"

"I'm not distressed. Just concerned. I know a little more about Mila Barnes now."

Liam narrowed his gaze. "Meaning what?"

"Meaning she's got *runner* written all over her. I don't want to see you get hurt. I don't want to see Shaylee get hurt. Not again."

Liam swore. "So let me get this straight. Now that I've jumped back on the *horse*—which is exactly what you advised me to do—you're having second thoughts."

"Not about you getting back on the horse."

"You don't know her that well, Slade. You told me that yourself."

"No. But I do read people pretty well. She's having second thoughts about moving here."

"Wouldn't you after what she's gone through? I told you Ledbetter's been riding her ass since she started at the PPB. He's dragging her down like a boat anchor. All these incidents are intercepting and it's going to be her demise."

Slade sighed. "Yeah, I get that. Tennant knows there's a problem. It's not the first time Ledbetter's caused issues. His grandfather and a couple of his uncles are all former cops with the bureau. Tennant's in a rock and a hard place but he's looking for a way out of it."

"That doesn't make it right."

"No, it doesn't. But it is what it is. How's Shaylee?"

"Stuffy nose and a slight fever. She's sleeping."

"Tell her I'll bring her some ice cream tomorrow."

"Okay. Everything okay with Ella?"

Slade grimaced. "She's crabbier than a grizzly bear and exhausted between pregnancy, working at the hospital and planning the wedding. Hopefully once the wedding is over, things will settle down. I'm worried about her."

Liam felt a little guilty for not staying more involved with Slade's situation. "If there's any way I can help, let me know."

"Will do."

At that moment, Sammy bounded down the stairs.

Liam's curiosity piqued and he looked his brother's partner in the eye. "Everything okay?"

"It's cool. Some of what she gave us panned out. We'll see what happens."

That was good news.

Both Slade and Sammy left and Liam went back to Shaylee.

14

Halfway through the day Sunday, Mila got a phone call from Captain Tennant. When she saw his number pop up on her phone, she started sweating profusely. Was he calling to fire her?

She supposed he probably wouldn't fire her over the phone. He'd want to do it in person.

Still…

After several rings, she knew she had to take the call. There was just no getting around it. Bracing herself, she greeted him.

"Barnes? Tennant here," he said, as though she didn't already know that. "I'm here at the precinct. I need to speak with you today. I'm only here until three. Head in as soon as you can."

Sweat turned to the chills. She had no choice but to accept the request.

Hanging up, she contemplated whether to wear her uniform or not. Technically she wasn't on shift for hours. Not only that, if he fired her, she wouldn't be on shift at all.

Choosing a pair of jeans and a nice blouse, she got ready and headed in to face her punishment. As luck would have it, she ran into Ledbetter in the parking lot. He had clearly been summoned, too. And he did not look happy.

"What did you do?" he demanded.

In no mood to get into it with him, she ignored him and continued on her way to Tennant's office. He was on the phone when she stopped in front of his doorway. He indicated for her to hang on. Taking a seat just outside the door, she tried to calm her erratic heartbeat. She'd never been fired in her life. Even as a teenager. Whenever she'd left a job, it had been by choice.

Until now.

"I hope you're happy. You should have kept your mouth shut," Ledbetter said, sitting down a few seats away.

"I don't know what you're talking about." She pretended to look through her phone.

"I suppose you didn't say something to someone that's got Tennant on our asses?"

"I didn't have to say anything, Ledbetter. People saw you in action. If you're in trouble, blame yourself, not me."

He snorted. "I may get a slap on the wrist, but you're done here. I heard about your little stunt yesterday. What were you thinking?"

She wasn't about to dignify the question with an answer. Fortunately, Tennant chose that moment to appear in front of his office door.

Both Mila and Ledbetter stood.

"You sit," Tennant said, giving Ledbetter a warning look. "I'll be with you in a minute."

Clearly surprised, Ledbetter dropped back into his chair.

Tennant gestured for Mila to follow him into his office. Once they were inside, he shut the door behind them. "Sit down."

This time the chair across from his desk was clear. She took a seat uneasily.

"We spoke a little over a week ago. Do you remember that, Barnes?"

She nodded.

"And when we spoke, I asked you about your situation with Ledbetter. I asked you about the report he wrote up regarding the Kendall case. Do you remember that, too?"

"Yes, sir."

"It's my understanding now, that the report Ledbetter filed is inaccurate. What do you have to say about that?"

She knew better than to avoid his gaze so she held eye contact steadily even though he made her want to shrivel. "The report was correct for the most part."

"So Ledbetter didn't leave you in a dangerous situation to fend for yourself until it was too late?"

She opened her mouth to speak, then shut it again when his gaze narrowed.

"I run a very tight ship here, Barnes," he went on. "Bullying, hazing, harassing—none of that's tolerated here. Do you understand me?"

"Yes, sir."

"You should have reported a problem when it first started. Now you've gotten yourself into a very precarious situation."

She merely nodded.

He folded his hands in front of him and stared at her for a few nerve-wracking seconds. "I'm not going to get into it any further with you regarding Ledbetter. He'll be dealt with appropriately. As for you, if I didn't have so many of your co-workers swearing to me that you're worth taking a chance on, I'd toss you out of here on your ass right now." His dark eyes were full of disbelief and anger as he pinned her with a stare. "What you did yesterday was irresponsible, unprofessional and reckless. You put yourself in a very dangerous situation that could have ended much worse than it did."

"I realize that, sir. At the time, I didn't know it was Vanessa Kendall that left the note on my door—"

He lifted his hand to silence her. "I've already heard the story from Haynes." Leaning back in his chair, he let her stew in the awkward silence that followed. She was thankful when he started speaking again. "You're ex-military, Barnes. So am I. As one soldier to another, I expect better from you."

The arrow hit its mark and she shriveled a little more.

He sat up straight and opened a file folder. "I'm taking you off the graveyard shift. You're working days now so I can keep a better eye on you. Do you have a problem with that?"

Surprised, she shook her head.

"You'll start tomorrow. Eight AM. You're with Brubaker now. He's a good kid with a good head on his shoulders. You two should work well together." He turned the file folder around and shoved a pen her way. "That being said, this is a write-up for you—a warning, so to speak. If anything like yesterday ever happens again, you're out. You understand me?"

She nodded solemnly, knowing better than to look too eager. She now had a black mark on her record.

"Good. Sign this and get out of here."

She quickly did as she was told. When she was finished, she made a beeline for the door. Just as she stepped through it, Tennant bellowed from behind her. "Ledbetter, get in here!"

Ledbetter gave her a dirty look as he sidestepped her and disappeared into Tennant's office.

She didn't wait around to see what happened. She took off for the parking lot.

Sammy was just exiting his truck as she reached her own car.

"Everything okay?" he asked, joining her beside her vehicle.

"Yes and no. I got my ass handed to me. But I still have a job. I'm on days now with Brubaker."

"I see that as a good thing," Sammy figured, leaning against her SUV. "Bru's a good kid."

"I like him. I think we'll work fine together." She glanced toward the precinct. "I have a bad feeling Ledbetter's getting fired right now."

"That's even an even better thing. It's a long time coming."

"Do you have anything new on the Kendall case?"

"Not that I can share. We're working some different angles."

She was a little disappointed that he couldn't let her in on whatever they had but she knew better than to push. She'd already gotten into enough trouble. "Thank you for whatever you said to Tennant. I'm pretty sure you single-handedly saved my job."

"I didn't say anything that wasn't true." He straightened. "Can you do me a favor?"

"Um, yeah. Pretty much anything after what you've done for me."

"I saw you and Liam the other day. I know this is none of my business but the Colsons are like family to me." He gave her a serious look. "He went through some really bad crap with his ex, Mila. I don't even think his family knows how bad it got for him."

She knew where this conversation was going. She didn't bother trying to stop it. She figured he had a right to say his piece.

"All I'm trying to say is be careful."

"You think I'm bad for him."

"Not at all. I think you know I respect the hell out of you."

"I hear a *but* in there."

"But he's had a tough time getting back on his feet. Don't knock him on his ass again."

Surprisingly, the warning didn't offend her. "What if he knocks me on mine?"

"Then he'll answer to me." He gave her a

wink and walked away.

. . .

Liam made some soup for Shaylee, which she made a face at. "I hate soup, Daddy. I want something else."

Since she'd arrived at his apartment the day before, she'd been finicky and cranky. She was feeling better but she was still out of sorts. He was doing his best to be patient with her but he was running low on tolerance at this point. "What else sounds good?"

"McDonald's."

He gave her a look. "We're not going to McDonald's."

"Mommy uses her phone and they bring the food to us," she informed him, making room so Lucky could cuddle up next to her on the couch. She was in a pair of pink, footed pajamas and she tucked her feet underneath her and clutched her prized stuffed frog, Furley, under her arm as she stared at Liam hopefully.

"I'm not Mommy. I don't have anything like that on my phone."

"You could get something like it. Pam has the same thing."

The mention of Pam grated on his nerves and he bit his tongue before anything came out that he was going to regret. "We've got food here in the apartment. Besides McDonald's what sounds good?"

"That's it," she whined, her eyes filling with tears. "I feel yucky and I want McDonald's."

He frowned at her. Usually she wasn't this argumentative. He reminded himself for what seemed like the millionth time, that she didn't feel good. Before he could say anything else, someone knocked on the door.

"Can I get it?" she asked hopefully, already sliding to her feet. "Maybe it's Uncle Slade. He promised me ice cream."

"Stay put," he ordered, walking over to the door and opening it. Slade wasn't on the doorstep. Mila was. She must have noticed the distressed look on his face because she frowned. "Are you okay?"

"Mila!" Before he could stop his daughter, she ran across the floor and leapt at Mila, who fortunately had good reflexes and caught her.

"Whoa! Slow down there."

"I haven't seen you in a long time. I thought maybe you moved away like Amber did."

"I still live upstairs." Mila grinned and set Shaylee back on her feet. "I thought you were sick. You look okay to me."

"I am sick. And I want McDonald's but Daddy won't get me any."

She scowled up at Liam and he frowned back. Sick or not, she was pushing his buttons. "I told you no. Go back to the couch and sit down. I don't want your fever coming back."

"I don't want to sit on the couch! I'm tired of resting!" She immediately turned on the water works and clung to Mila's leg.

Mila gave Liam a helpless look. "Sorry. I guess I came by at a bad time."

"You didn't. We're just having a difference of opinion." He pried Shaylee from her leg and shook his head as he all but dragged the child, kicking and screaming, back to the couch. He sat her down and pointed his finger sternly in her face. "Stop it right now. If you don't, you're going to your room for a nap."

She stopped kicking at him but she continued to cry.

He pinched the bridge of his nose in frustration.

"McDonald's isn't all that great. I've got a better idea." Mila was there suddenly, standing beside him. She crouched down in front of Shaylee, who continued to bawl. "When I was your age and I didn't feel good, my mom always made me something special. Do you want to know what?"

Shaylee's sobbing slowed a bit but didn't stop entirely.

"You have to stop crying or I can't tell you."

Swiping at the tears on her cheeks, Shaylee quieted down after a moment. She sniffled a bit, then observed Mila curiously. "What did she make you?"

"Special, magic cinnamon toast."

"Magic?" Shaylee was instantly intrigued.

"Yep. Would you like me to make you some? I have the ingredients right upstairs."

Shaylee sniffled again as she nodded eagerly. "Can she, Daddy?"

Liam stood there in awe. He had no idea how he'd lost control of the situation, or how Mila had gotten it back, so easily.

Mila stood up straight and gave him a questioning glance. "It's just a little sugar, cinnamon and butter on white toast. Is that okay?" she asked for his ears only.

"It's fine," he readily agreed. "I have the stuff here. You don't have to go upstairs."

While he re-situated his daughter on the couch, Mila made the "magic cinnamon toast" and added a glass of milk to the tray before she carried it toward the couch and set it on the coffee table.

Shaylee smiled as she viewed the concoction. "I've never had magic cinnamon toast. Can I watch a cartoon while I eat it?" She glanced Liam's way.

He nodded and reached for the remote. When Shaylee was happily immersed in her meal, he joined Mila at the kitchen counter where she was tidying up. "Are you sure you don't have any kids of your own?"

She grinned halfway. "Nope. But I was a child once myself."

He grunted. "So was I. My mom would have spanked my butt if I'd behaved that way."

"Mine might have, too," she agreed, chuckling. "But she would have made me the magic cinnamon toast, too."

"Did Shaylee disturb you with her screaming?" He suddenly wondered how she'd managed to show up at his door at just the right time.

"No. I was just coming in. I had a meeting with Tennant down at the precinct."

He leaned against the counter. She didn't look too upset so he could only assume she hadn't gotten fired. "Dare I ask what happened?"

"I got my ass chewed." She shrugged sheepishly. "I expected it. I screwed up. I no longer have to worry about Ledbetter. I think he got fired right after I left."

"It's about time. You want to celebrate?"

She grinned. "Nah. I feel kind of bad. The guy's an idiot. He's definitely not police officer material. That sucks for him because he comes from a long line of cops."

"He's a male chauvinist pig," he reminded her. "No profession looks kindly on that these days."

"True. Fortunately, I don't have to deal with him anymore."

"Thank God for that."

"And I got moved to days."

"You did?"

"Yeah." She frowned. "Tennant made it sound like part of my punishment for what happened yesterday. He told me it's so he can keep a close eye on me. I'm with Brubaker now. Carter. Have you met him?"

"We've crossed paths before. He seems like an okay guy."

"I like him." She glanced at her watch. "I should probably get out of your hair. I know you have to work in the morning." She paused. "What are you going to do with Shaylee? Will she be able to go to school?"

"Undetermined. I'll take her temperature in the morning and if she's got a fever or still feels rotten, I'll figure something out. My mother's usually more than willing to step in."

She nodded and walked over to the couch. Shaylee was still eating her toast happily. "Bye, Shaylee."

"Why do you have to go? We could watch a cartoon."

Liam sensed his daughter was about to start up the waterworks again and nipped the situation in the bud. "She's got work in the morning and so do I. You've got school. Finish up your toast and you're going to take a bath."

Shaylee started to pout again. "I'm not going to bed yet. It's not even seven."

"If you get sassy, you'll go to bed right now. I'm going to walk Mila upstairs. Be good while I'm gone."

Shaylee sniffled again but apparently thought better of taking things further. She sat back on the couch and gave the cartoon on the television her full attention again.

"I can make it upstairs on my own," Mila said when they were alone in the hall.

He reached for her, setting his hands on her hips and pulling her toward him. He planted his mouth firmly against hers, wasting no time in deepening the kiss when she opened.

She melted against him, her arms wrapping around his neck. "Or maybe I can't."

He grinned against her lips. "Thank you."

"For what?"

"For diverting the impending tragedy in there. If you hadn't shown up with your magic toast, she would have had a complete meltdown and I would have been pulling out my hair right about now."

She laughed. "I have no doubt you would have figured out something but I'm glad I could help."

"Me, too." He rubbed his nose against hers. "I wish I could see you again tonight. But with her in the apartment…"

"I get it. Take care of her and we'll talk later."

He gave her another very deep, very thorough kiss. Then he let her go and waited until she was up the stairs before he went back inside his apartment.

15

When Mila got into work on Monday morning, it didn't take her long to get the rundown on what had happened to Ledbetter. The rumor mill was in full swing. She heard a few different versions of what happened to him before she finally got what she figured out was the real story from Brubaker.

They started out their rounds with some small talk and an apology from her. "I'm sorry about Finley. I hope you're not upset that you're forced to partner up with me. I know you guys got along pretty good."

Brubaker—who incidentally, was in the passenger seat—shrugged his shoulders. "It's cool. I'm pretty easy going. And to be honest with you, I plan to go up for Detective soon. That's my passion. I'm just getting experience right now, paying my dues."

She admired his perseverance. "Yeah, me, too. Because of what happened over the weekend, I may be paying them longer than anyone else."

He grinned. "I heard about that. At least you didn't get fired like Ledbetter."

She grimaced. "I heard rumors this morning but they were all different."

"He got the ax. Finley's back on the desk and she saw him leave yesterday. He was pretty upset." He shrugged. "He's gotten a lot of complaints over the past several months. Everybody knew his days were numbered."

She kept her commentary to herself. At this point, she was starting fresh and she wanted to have a clean slate.

Working with Brubaker was Heaven compared to her days with Ledbetter. They did a few traffic stops. The day was pretty quiet.

When her shift was over, she stepped into Sammy and Slade's cubicle. Slade wasn't there but Sammy was hard at work at his desk. She knocked on the cubicle wall.

"Hey," he said, glancing up. "How was your first day shift?"

"Good. I just thought I'd see if anything is

new on the Kendall case."

He shook his head and indicated the chair near his desk. "Sit down for a minute. I was going to look you up anyway. I have a couple of questions for you about Vanessa Kendall."

She dropped into the chair. "I told you everything she told me."

"Are you sure you don't remember her mentioning anywhere she might hide out? No relatives? Friends?"

She shook her head. "I wish I could help more. I was pretty skeptical of her story at first so I don't think she completely trusted me."

"I figured as much." He scraped a hand over his jaw. "I'm going to head over to Edith Crawford's again right now. You want to tag along? Slade's at an appointment with Ella so I'm going solo."

"Really?" She did her best to contain her excitement. "What about Tennant? I don't want to get in more trouble."

"I ran it by him first. It's basically shadowing. You want to be a detective someday, right?"

"Yes! Heck yes!" She was on her feet instantly.

He chuckled and grabbed his keys.

The ride to Edith Crawford's took around twenty-five minutes. When they pulled up in front of her house, it was just after five-thirty.

"I don't have to tell you to let me do the talking. Like I said, consider this shadowing," he warned.

She nodded and followed him up the walk. When he rapped on the door, she waited behind him silently.

The older woman who answered looked to be in her late fifties. She had graying, blond hair and wide, blue eyes. She was short and a little on the hefty side. When she saw Sammy, she smiled but Mila noticed right away that the smile didn't quite reach her eyes. "Detective Haynes. I wasn't expecting you again today."

"Mrs. Crawford. I know. I'm sorry I didn't call first but I have a few more questions for you. This is Officer Mila Barnes. She's along for the ride."

Mrs. Crawford seemed a little conflicted, but she eventually opened the door and they walked into the house.

Mila noticed immediately there was a pleasant smell in the air. Some kind of fragrant, spicy scent.

"I'm just putting my dinner on. Do you mind stepping into the kitchen? I don't want it to burn."

"Not at all," Sammy said. He and Mila followed her down a hallway and into a spacious, yet old school kitchen. The appliances were brown and the walls were in need of a new paint job. The room resembled something straight out of the seventies.

Mrs. Crawford went to work stirring something on the stove. "So what's this about? I already told you everything I know about the Kendalls."

"I realize you've been very cooperative. I just have some questions for you regarding your timeline," Sammy began, peering into a small, black notebook he removed from his coat pocket. "I know you said you've witnessed the Kendalls arguing often over the past several months. Tell me again when the last time was that you saw Vanessa Kendall at home."

Mrs. Crawford set her spoon aside and gave that some thought. "As I mentioned, I saw her right after Mr. Kendall was released from jail. That was Monday, I believe."

"And after that?"

"Trash day is Tuesday. I saw her then, too. She pushed out the can like she always does."

"After that?" he prodded.

"I saw lights on in the house late into the night Tuesday. I could see clearly that they weren't getting along." She turned down the burner and pivoted to face him. "That's the way they always were. I felt really bad for her. She was a sweet woman. She tried so hard to make the marriage work. I told her a couple of times what I thought about him. She just didn't have the backbone to leave him."

"You told her you thought she should?" Sammy asked.

"Yes, a couple of times when we ran into each other in the yard. I know it wasn't my business but I just hated seeing her battered that way. It wasn't right. Nobody deserves to be treated like that. He was a mean, cussed man."

"Did you ever see Vanessa Kendall get violent with her husband in return?"

"No. I think she was scared to death of him. That's just my opinion of course, but it's the way I saw things."

He returned his notebook to his pocket. "I appreciate you taking the time to speak to me again. It goes without saying that if you think of anything else that might help us, please call."

"Of course." She walked them to the foyer.

Mila trailed behind. Just as she was nearing the front door, she fumbled with her phone and it fell to the ground. She leaned over to pick it up and at the same time, her eyes landed on something that was lying on the floor near a well-used leather couch.

A dark blue sweatshirt.

All in one moment, Mila's skin began to chill.

"Are you alright?" Mrs. Crawford asked

cautiously.

Mila snatched up her phone quickly. "I'm fine. I dropped my phone." She gave the woman a forced smile and followed Sammy outside. She didn't speak until they were both back in his truck and he had the engine running.

"Sammy?"

"Yeah?"

"Did you see the sweatshirt on the floor in the living room?"

He glanced at her as he pulled out into traffic. "No. What sweatshirt?"

"It was a dark blue hoodie. It was lying on the floor near the couch in the living room."

He shrugged. "What about it?"

She swallowed hard. "When I saw Vanessa Kendall the other day, she was wearing a dark blue hoodie."

He narrowed his eyes. "Lots of people have dark blue hoodies, Mila. I have a couple at home myself."

She could hear the skepticism in his voice. She braced an arm against the windowsill and went silent.

"Why are you so quiet?"

"I'm not," she responded solemnly.

"You are. You're that upset over a sweatshirt?"

She met his gaze. "Do you want the truth?"

"I would prefer it."

"That woman's strange. There's something off about her."

"In what way?"

That was just it, she wasn't sure. She thought for a moment. "She kept referring to Vanessa Kendall in past tense. The woman's not dead, she's just missing."

"A lot of people do that in situations like this. She probably feels that way because it's been a few days since she's seen her."

"Has her story altered at all?"

"No. That's one of the reasons I went back and requestioned her today. I wanted to be sure she didn't change anything." He pulled to a stop when they reached the precinct. "Listen, I know you're on edge about this whole thing and it's no wonder why. I probably shouldn't have taken you with me today."

"I'm glad you did," she relented, telling herself he was likely right about Edith Crawford. She was just being paranoid. "I'd love to tag along whenever I can. I'm hoping to be a detective myself someday."

"I think you will be. Just keep your nose clean."

They both exited the vehicle. Mila's SUV was parked nearby so while he went back into the building, she headed for home. When she got there, she grabbed her mail and went straight to her apartment. Liam was on shift at the fire station so she didn't bother stopping by to say hi. Instead, she made herself a frozen dinner and sat down in front of the television. She flipped channels for a while, finally deciding on the evening news. When she was finished eating, she loaded the dishwasher. All the while, she just couldn't shake the unsettled feeling she'd had when she'd bent down in Edith Crawford's home and caught sight of the blue hoodie.

Sighing, she shut the television off and picked up her phone. She dialed Reid's number.

He answered on the first ring. "I was just thinking about you. What's up?"

"You busy?"

"No. I just got home. I've got a burger cooking. What's on your mind?"

She hadn't been honest with her brother about her troubles at work. She figured now was as good a time as any. She filled him in on what had happened with Ledbetter. She also told him about Michael Kendall and the situation with his wife.

When she was done, he audibly sighed and let out a curse. "What a dick. I'm glad the creep got canned."

"Yeah, I'm glad to be rid of him. This thing with Vanessa Kendall is really bothering me though. I went with Sammy to re-question one of her neighbors and I saw a sweatshirt on the floor in the woman's house that looked an awful lot like the one Vanessa was wearing when I met her at Fred Griffin Park."

"Did it have some sort of distinct design on it?"

"No."

"So it was just a blue sweatshirt."

She heard the skepticism in his voice and it reminded her of Sammy's. She scowled. "It was a hoodie."

"That's not exactly distinct, sis. A lot of people have blue hoodies. I have—"

"Do not tell me you have one yourself. That's what Sammy said."

"So you told him what you saw." It wasn't a question.

"I told him."

"He's in charge of the investigation, right?"

"He is." She stared up at the ceiling, frustrated.

"Then it's his call. If he thought it was worth looking into, he'd do it. I'd be real careful about stepping on his toes. He's probably your biggest ally."

"I know." Defeated, she propped the phone between her ear and her shoulder. "The thing is, I sense something off about this woman."

"Just because she has a blue sweatshirt in her house?"

"No. Not just that." She thought things over for a moment. "I don't know what it is about her but it's something. I mean she mentioned that she told Vanessa Kendall numerous times to leave her husband. That's pretty nervy. The way Vanessa talked about her, they weren't close. Would you tell someone to leave their husband that you didn't know that well?"

"Probably not but you have no way of knowing what their true relationship was. You're going solely on what Vanessa Kendall told you. She might be a liar. In fact, considering the situation she's in, she probably is."

She couldn't discount the theory. "So you think I should let things lie."

"Absolutely. You're not a detective. You're not on the case. Not only that, you've gotten yourself into enough trouble recently. You're liable to lose your job if you keep going rogue like this."

"I'm not going rogue," she snapped irritably.

"Call it what you want. So how's the fireman?"

Her skin warmed when she thought about Liam. "He's fine."

"So in other words, you're still seeing him." He chuckled.

"What's so funny about that?"

"Nothing's funny. I had a feeling you were going to lean back in his direction. As flustered as you were the other day, I sensed he's gotten under your skin."

"He has not," she denied, even though she knew she was lying.

"Keep telling yourself that." She heard a ding in the background. "Listen, my dinner is done. You want me to call you back later?"

"Nah. I'm going to go to bed. I start early in the morning now that I'm on days."

"Stay out of trouble, Mila."

She mumbled an agreement and hung up. Still unsettled, she went to the bedroom and pulled some pajamas out. She did her nightly ritual of washing her face and brushing her teeth. Then she lay there in the dark, staring up at the ceiling.

For an hour, she tossed and turned. Aggravated, she gave up on trying to sleep. She just couldn't stop thinking about Edith Crawford and the odd feeling she'd gotten while she'd been in the woman's house. Her instincts were telling her something was wrong.

Sitting up, she raked a hand through her hair. Then she reached for her phone. She went through her contacts until she found Sammy's phone number. It was after ten. He was probably asleep. If she woke him, he'd be pissed.

She second-guessed herself.

Swearing, she set her phone down. What was she doing? Reid was right. She needed to mind her own business.

Vanessa Kendall's battered and beaten face flashed in her mind and she grimaced.

After giving the matter a few more minutes of thought, she grabbed some clothes and quickly dressed. Then she snatched up her phone and service revolver and went for her car keys.

There was no harm in doing a quick drive-by past Edith Crawford's house. If it was dark and all looked peaceful, she'd just come back home and go to bed.

She was in her SUV before she could talk herself out of what she was doing. Traffic was light so she entered the neighborhood just after eleven.

Most of the houses on the tree-lined street were dark at this hour. The area looked a bit more ominous than it had in the daytime, especially when she reached the Kendall home, where there was still crime scene tape stretched out across the yard.

She slowed down and glanced at Edith Crawford's home. It was dark, too, not a light on in the place.

The hairs on the back of Mila's neck stood on

end. She continued on by the house, knowing she couldn't just idle right in front of it. Someone would definitely call the police.

Reaching the end of the block, she turned left and went around to the alley. It was a narrow opening with detached garages lining both sides.

She knew Edith Crawford had cameras focused on her backyard. She had no way of knowing how many other neighbors had the same security measures. She didn't want to get herself into a predicament where she was caught on surveillance.

She slowed to a stop and turned off her lights. She knew one house on the block for sure didn't have cameras.

The Kendall house.

If she wanted to get a better look at Edith Crawford's place, that was where she was going to start.

Making sure her weapon was handy, she left her vehicle and crept down the dark alley. A couple of residents had motion lights so she found herself hurrying faster once they activated. When she reached the Kendall home, she peered around the corner of the garage and through the back gate. She squinted as something caught her eye.

A dim light. It was coming from inside the house.

She stopped breathing for a minute and continued to peer into the home.

The light began to move. A flashlight, she realized. Someone was inside the house, creeping around with a flashlight.

Her blood ran cold instantly.

"What the hell are you doing?"

The male voice startled her so badly she almost screamed. Turning abruptly, she found Sammy standing behind her in the alley, a frown on his face.

No, *frown* was an understatement. He looked angry as hell.

She was a little angry in her own right. "You just scared the hell out of me!" The admonishment came out in a loud whisper.

"What are you doing here, Barnes?"

Her heart pounding erratically inside her chest, she exhaled painfully. "Something's wrong here. I just know it. I couldn't sleep so I thought I'd do a quick drive-by."

"Are you *trying* to get fired?"

She felt a little like a child being scolded. "I think Vanessa Kendall is in Edith Crawford's house. Or at the very least, she was." She pointed toward the Kendall's backyard. "I just saw someone moving around inside the Kendall house, too. Someone with a flashlight."

They both peered into the home. All was dark

now.

"I saw someone, Sammy. I swear it." A thought occurred to her and she narrowed her eyes at him. "Why are you here? You acted like you didn't believe me earlier — like I was barking up the wrong tree."

He gave her a look. "It had nothing to do with me believing you. A blue sweatshirt lying on the floor in someone's living room is not probable cause. There's no way I could have gotten a warrant with just that."

Suddenly she caught on. "So you're here looking for more." She felt oddly vindicated.

He gave her another stern stare. "You're way out of line here and you're interfering in my investigation. If Tennant finds out about this, he's going to have your head and mine."

The realization that he was right ate at her. She glanced back toward the Kendall house. "I saw a light moving around in there. Can't we at least check it out?"

"No. You can get back in your car and go home. *We* are not doing anything."

"Are you going to keep watching?"

"Barnes, go home," he repeated. "That's a direct order."

She had no smoice but to do as he said. Reluctantly, she turned and headed up the alley. Once she reached her car, she turned back in his direction. He was gone.

Cursing the fact that she had no authority whatsoever, she climbed into her vehicle. She glanced down at her phone and saw she had a missed call from Reid. She hit the button to return the call.

"I suggest you set the phone down right now." The voice came from behind her and it was not Sammy's. It belonged to woman. She recognized it right away. Turning her head, she found herself staring into the deep, dark depths of Vanessa Kendall's eyes.

A chill shot up her spine and she swallowed hard. The woman had a gun pointed right at the side of Mila's head.

"Hang up that call," Vanessa hissed.

Mila did as she was told.

"Now give me your gun."

Mila hesitated, knowing she was signing her own death warrant if she gave up her weapon.

"Give me your fucking gun. I've got no problem shooting you right here if you don't."

"If you shoot me right here, someone will hear you. I'm not the only cop in this alley tonight."

"I'm well aware of that, Officer Barnes. I just watched Detective Haynes drive off in his truck."

Mila instantly felt her hope dwindle. She'd gotten herself into this mess and now she was going to have to get herself out of it. Alone.

Trying to buy herself some time, she made no move to relinquish her weapon. "You did kill your husband."

Vanessa snorted. "The cheating bastard had it coming.   I don't feel one ounce of guilt for putting him out of his misery. I did the world a favor."

"I saw your sweatshirt in your neighbor's house."

"I know you did. That wasn't planned. I dropped it on my way down the stairs. The old biddy didn't even know I was in the house. If you'd said something while you were there..." Vanessa chuckled. "But you didn't."

Mila shivered as she thought of Vanessa watching them from somewhere in the shadows of Edith Crawford's house. "Why were you there?"

Vanessa ignored her question, poking her in the side of her head with the gun. "Give me your weapon. Then we're going to take a walk."

Knowing she had no choice, Mila unclipped her weapon and reluctantly gave it to Vanessa, who shoved it into the back of her pants. "Now get out of the car and follow me. Don't make a sound."

Mila did as she was told.   She had to buy herself some time. She knew her call to Reid had connected—not for long, but hopefully for long enough. Maybe he would call for help. In the meantime, she had to play along with this charade until she had an opportunity to defend herself. She'd done so with Michael Kendall and he'd outweighed his wife by at least fifty pounds.

Vanessa kept low and to the left, her hand on Mila's arm. She seemed to know exactly where all the motion lights were located and was able to avoid them. When they reached Edith Crawford's house, she dragged Mila up the back steps and onto the dark porch. The back door was unlocked and a moment later, they were both inside.

Vanessa didn't bother turning on the lights. She used her flashlight to illuminate the kitchen. That's when Mila saw Edith Crawford lying in the middle of the floor, blood pooling around her. Her eyes were wide open and she was staring at the ceiling. There was a kitchen knife sticking out of her chest. Clearly she was dead.

Mila started to sweat.

"The old bitch should have minded her own business. She was always watching—always putting in her two cents." Vanessa shook her head in disgust. "She knew what I did. She knew I killed Michael. She agreed to cover for me at first. Her own husband was a rotten bastard so she felt sorry for me. We worked out a plan together. I would hide out for a while, act like I was scared to death. Then I'd contact the police and plead my innocence. I knew her cameras weren't pointed anywhere near my house. It sounded good when I told you to ask for the footage, didn't it? I was very convincing."

Mila felt sick to her stomach as she realized she'd fallen for this woman's act. Every bit of it.

"As you can probably guess—" Vanessa went on. "—the bitch changed her mind. The more the cops came around, the more frazzled she became. I knew she was going to turn on me. I had no choice but to take care of her."

This woman was clearly deranged. "You could have claimed self-defense, Vanessa. None of this was necessary."

"Don't you tell me that! I tried reasoning with you that day in the park. You were going to turn me in."

"I had no choice. It's my job."

"Fuck your job. Is it worth dying for?"

The question echoed in Mila's head several times.

"Just shut up and go downstairs to the basement. It's soundproof down there."

The meaning in those words haunted Mila as they moved through the hallway, toward the basement door. She knew she had to do something to save herself now. Once they were in the basement, all bets were off.

"Hurry up!" Vanessa jabbed her with the gun again.

Instead of following the order and going through the basement door, Mila did a quick pivot, used a very effective martial arts move, and knocked the gun from Vanessa's hand.

Vanessa let out a shriek and fell backward against the wall nearby. Mila dove for the weapon she'd dislodged. Vanessa grabbed her by the foot, stopping her just before she reached it. "You stupid, stupid bitch!" Suddenly Mila's own service weapon was digging into the skin of her temple.

She went limp, knowing there was nothing she could do to help herself now.

The gunshot rang out, echoing throughout the room. Mila felt the spatter of blood as it exploded above her head. The gun that had been poking her fell to the ground and Vanessa Kendall collapsed on top of her, bleeding profusely from a bullet wound in the middle of her forehead.

A little panicked at being pinned, Mila fought, shoving the woman's body aside. The smell of blood assaulted her nostrils as she peered into the darkness across the room and her eyes locked with Sammy's. He stood in the doorway, his gun still drawn and ready to shoot.

16

Hours later, Mila sat in a chair across from Captain Tennant, in his office.

She'd been allowed to shower — to change out of her bloody clothing. Now she had to face her punisher.

Tennant had been eerily silent while Sammy briefed him on everything that had happened. Then Sammy had left, shutting the door behind him. Now, Tennant was staring at Mila as if he wanted to throttle her.

Leaning back in his chair, he shook his head at her. "I don't know whether to fire you, or promote you, Barnes. What the hell is wrong with you?"

She sat there silently, really having no explanation for him.

"What you did was dangerous, irresponsible and downright stupid." He paused. "I feel like I'm on a literal repeat with you. Even after I warned you..." He shook his head and his words trailed off.

She fidgeted uncomfortably.

"But you've got good instincts."

Surprised, she raised her head.

"I'm not rewarding you. Not by a long shot. You're damn lucky you're alive right now. If your brother hadn't called Haynes and told him what he heard over the phone..." Tennant continued to frown. "You're on leave until I figure out what the hell to do with you. Go home."

She got out of her chair and left the office wearily. Sammy was waiting for her when she hit the lobby. He wasn't smiling, he wasn't frowning. He just gave her a questioning arch of the brow.

"He didn't fire me. Not yet."

"That's good. If he were going to, he would have." He followed her through the front doors and out into the parking lot. "For what it's worth, I believed you earlier. When you saw that sweatshirt, I knew something wasn't right myself. That's why I was there tonight. I was in the house next door, checking things out, when your brother called me. By the way, you'd better call him as soon as you get home. I let him know you're still alive but he's upset."

She cringed at the intense tongue lashing she knew she was going to get from her brother. "I was wrong about Edith Crawford," she admitted lamely.

"Not really. She was covering for Vanessa Kendall. You saw something off about her and you acted on that instinct. I had the same one. That's why I kept going back there. I should have kept you in the loop and maybe none of this would have happened." He shrugged solemnly. "I got my ass chewed, too, if it makes you feel any better."

"It doesn't. Not really."

"Look, Barnes, you've got a future in law enforcement but you're going to have to reel yourself in. Study up on protocol and follow it. If you make it long enough, you'll be a great detective. And that's just a start."

She appreciated the praise. "Thank you."

"Don't thank me. We're both in deep shit right now."

She smiled halfway and they walked out to the parking lot together.

She called her brother while she drove home. Upset was quite an understatement when describing his mood. He was beside himself. After twenty minutes of assuring him she was okay, she finally got him off the phone, just as she was pulling to a stop in front of the Victorian.

She was surprised when Liam approached her before she even made it up the walk. He looked pretty alarmed himself. "You just scared the hell out of me."

She could see clearly he wasn't exaggerating. The fact that he was concerned about her warmed her cold bones a little. "What are you doing home? You're supposed to be at work."

"Why do you think I'm home? Slade told me what happened. I got someone to cover for me."

She felt a little emotional all the sudden, which was odd. She really wasn't the emotional type.

He muttered an oath and pulled her against his chest.

Her skin warmed instantly. She felt a whole lot better tucked into his embrace.

"Are you okay?" he spoke the words into her hair quietly.

"I'm okay," she managed. "I think I just need to settle down a bit. I know Shaylee's at your place but do you think it would be a big deal if I hung out with you for a bit?" She really didn't feel like being alone.

"She's spending the night at my mom's.

Come on."

They went to his apartment. He insisted on making her something to eat even though she wasn't all that hungry. She merely picked at the sandwich he made her.

He took a few minutes to shower and change clothes. She curled up on his bed with the remote in her hand to wait for him. Lucky curled up next to her and the cat's presence was oddly comforting. By the time Liam came back into the bedroom she was dozing on and off.

He took the remote from her hand and turned off the television. Then he shut the light off and slid in beside her. He didn't say anything, just pulled her back against his chest and wrapped his arms around her.

Content, she allowed herself to fall into a dreamless sleep.

Halfway through the night, they both awoke. It didn't take long for things to heat up. When they came together, it was slow and easy, familiar. She didn't want the moment to end so she held on as long as she physically could. When her body came apart, she exhaled deeply and moaned into the pillow nearby.

He followed suit, burying his head in her neck.

Afterward, he rolled, taking her with him and tucking her snugly against his side. She heard his breathing even out and knew he was asleep again. Slumber didn't come as easy to her this time. She lay there for nearly an hour before her eyes finally gave in and shut the world around her out.

When she awoke the next morning, sun was already filtering in through the window across the room. Glancing at the bedside clock, she realized it was just after seven AM.

She didn't move right away. She was warm and comfortable in Liam's arms and she was hesitant to let the feeling go.

"You okay?"

She turned at the sound of his sleepy voice in her ear. His gray eyes locked with hers and her breath caught. She knew at that moment she was in over her head. She was far more attached to him than she wanted to be.

"Mila?"

"I'm okay," she managed to get out. She raked a hand through her hair and turned onto her back, staring up at the ceiling. She knew better than to keep looking him in the eye.

Instead of peppering her with questions, he relaxed his head on the pillow next to hers and followed her gaze.

An awkward silence ensued and he finally sighed. "I'm going to have to go get Shaylee from my mom's."

"I know. I should go anyway." She started to sit up.

He reached for her, grasping her chin with his fingers gently. "I get the feeling you're pushing me away. All you have to do is tell me if you want me to back off."

Did she want that?

Everything in her life was suddenly very confusing. "I don't know what I want," she eventually admitted.

He sighed and let her go. "I know this thing with us has happened pretty fast, but I feel like we connect in a lot of ways. I haven't felt that way about anyone in…" He shrugged. "…a really long time. I know maybe you're not on the same page so I'm going to leave the ball in your court. Take some time and figure out what you're ready for. I'll be here when you do."

She wanted to tell him she didn't need time. She wanted to tell him she was head over heels for him—for his daughter, too. Instead, she nodded and climbed from his bed.

She moved through the day on autopilot. She still had unopened boxes in her apartment. Looking at them depressed her. She didn't want them there, yet she didn't feel at all like unpacking them. Instead, she called Reid, who wasn't as sympathetic to her situation as she would have liked.

"I warned you about everything you're upset about right now, Mila. I told you not to go rogue again. I warned you about alienating your allies at the bureau. And I warned you about sleeping with Liam Colson. I don't know what you want me to say to you now."

She didn't know what she wanted him to say, either.

"Listen," he said, his tone softening. "You're on leave for the time being. Why don't you come up north and spend a few days here? You like the mountain. We'll do some hiking. Whatever you want. It might help you clear your head."

"I'll think about it."

They disconnected and she tossed her phone down on the coffee table. Then she curled up in a corner of the couch and laid there, staring at the lifeless television screen across the room.

Hours went by before she finally dragged herself up and into the shower. After cleaning up, she did a load of laundry. Then she went down to the mailboxes and retrieved her mail.

As she stood there thumbing through bill after bill, she suddenly got a very strange feeling. The hairs on the back of her neck stood on end. She peered around the empty hallway, sensing she wasn't alone.

Yet there was nobody there.

A chill shot up her spine and she peered

around the corner at Liam's closed door. Nothing looked amiss. All was quiet.

Shrugging the sense of unease aside, she went back up to her apartment and shut the lights off. Then she went into her bedroom and climbed under the covers.

Mentally exhausted, she willed her mind to shut down. Just as she was dozing off, her cell phone rang from its charger next to the bed.

Cursing, she reached for it. The number flashing on the screen wasn't one she recognized. Cautiously, she greeted the caller.

At first, nobody responded.

She greeted the caller again, this time curtly.

"Is this Officer Barnes?" The voice was female and so quiet she could barely hear it.

Sitting up in her bed, Mila's gaze narrowed. "Yes. Who is this?"

There was a space of hesitation in the line. Then she heard a small hiccup. "Jana Whitfield. We met the other night when my house…" The girl's voice trailed off.

Instantly, Mila's heart thumped into overdrive. "I remember you, Jana. How can I help you?"

"I—I don't know. I just…" The girl's voice suddenly dissolved into a sob. "I shouldn't have called you. I don't know why I did."

Mila swung her feet over the side of the bed.

"I know why you did, Jana. Because you know I can help you. Are you at home? Do you want me to come there and we can talk?"

"No! Please don't! My mom—my brother—they don't know I'm calling you."

Afraid the girl was going to hang up, Mila backtracked. "Okay. I understand. Do you want to meet me somewhere? I can pick you up."

The girl answered Mila's question with one of her own. "Is it too late?"

Mila was instantly standing, already digging for whatever clean clothing was handy. "No. I can be there in fifteen minutes."

"No, I mean for me to—to tell you what really happened."

Stopping abruptly, Mila leaned against the dresser, sensing it was now or never with this girl. "No, Jana, it's not too late."

"That guy the other night—your partner. He told me to be sure about everything I said—that changing my story later would result in nobody believing me." Her voice shook and she sniffled audibly. "I wanted to tell the truth but I was so scared. And he just kept looking at me with cold eyes. I didn't know what to do."

Mila found herself cursing Ledbetter for what seemed like the millionth time. Pinching the bridge of her nose, she sat back down on the bed.

"I'm sorry you felt that way, Jana. It's not too late for you to tell me what really happened. I can help you if you let me."

Jana was quiet for a long time and Mila was a little worried she'd lost the teenager. Then she heard another hiccup. After that, Jana came clean. In a somewhat hysterical rush, she described everything that happened the night of the burglary, including a very violent sexual assault.

Mila felt sick for the teenager. Her stomach clenched as Jana finally dissolved into a fit of tears and stopped talking.

"I think you should talk to your mother, Jana. I know you don't want to—that you think you have something to be embarrassed about. You don't. What happened wasn't your fault. She'll understand that. You're going to need her support."

"She's going to be mad at me. I was the one who left the backdoor open. I was outside smoking." Jana continued to sob. "When I came back in, I forgot to lock it."

Mila sighed regretfully. "That doesn't make anything that happened your fault."

"It was so awful." Jana continued to hiccup. "I just keep seeing his face. I keep hearing his voice, smelling his breath…"

"Do you think you can describe him to one of

our sketch artists?"

Jana sniffled again. "Maybe." She was quiet for a moment. "I didn't go to the hospital. Does that mean there's no evidence?"

"Not necessarily. Do you still have the clothing you were wearing that night?" Mila was back to dragging clothes from her dresser again. She knew she wasn't going to be going back to bed at this point.

"I put them in a plastic grocery bag and hid them in my closet. I didn't want my mom to see them in the garbage."

Mila felt a sliver of hope. "That's good, Jana. It's good that you still have them. I'm going to need them. Do you think you can come down to the station and bring them to me? I know this is hard but I need to have you tell me what you just told me on record."

"Just you? Not your partner?"

"Just me," Mila assured her.

"Okay," the girl agreed hesitantly. "I need to talk to my mom first."

"You take your time. I'll be waiting for you both at the station."

Jana agreed and disconnected the call.

Mila immediately phoned the station. It was after eight in the evening and she knew Tennant wouldn't be there. She also knew she needed to follow protocol this time. The supervising officer on duty confirmed she should come into the station and they would handle the situation together.

Grabbing her car keys, she locked up her apartment and headed for her vehicle. Just as she was about to climb inside, a hand came around her from behind and slammed over her mouth hard enough to draw blood.

Struggling was second nature and she fought with everything she had.

Whoever was behind her used a defensive move to block her self-defense attack. She was slammed roughly up against her vehicle. The wind was immediately knocked out of her. She felt the gun at her waist poke her as it was lifted away from its holster.

"You fucking bitch," a male voice seethed in her ear. "Do you know what you've done to me?"

She recognized the voice immediately.

Ledbetter.

Her stomach rolled as she smelled the very distinct scent of alcohol on his breath.

"Stop fighting me," he warned. "If you attract any attention, you're going to regret it. You don't want your boyfriend and his pretty little girl to get mixed up in this mess you've made, do you?"

She knew he was talking about Liam—about

Shaylee. Fear clenched at her heart and she stopped fighting him. There was no way she was going to let him hurt either one of them.

"We're going to go for a little ride, sweetheart. Get in the car."

She made no move to obey him.

His grip on her arms tightened. "On the other hand, I don't mind grabbing them. Maybe they'd like to come along."

Knowing she had no choice, she let him manhandle her into the vehicle and over the gear shift. He snapped the locks into place before she could even think about trying to escape. Then he slid into the driver's seat and held out his hand. "Give me your keys—and your phone."

She helplessly slapped both items into his palm. "You're a cop, Ledbetter. What are you doing?"

He jammed the key into the ignition as he tossed her phone out the driver's side window. "I'm not a cop. Not anymore. Not thanks to you." His voice shook with anger and he pinned her with a glare that had her recoiling. He looked like a total stranger. His eyes were bloodshot and vacant. His mouth was turned down in a thin, evil scowl. "Tennant told my grandfather everything. I'm a disgrace now, thanks to you."

"I didn't do anything but tell the truth." She

swiped at the blood that was dripping from her lip.

"I was on the fast track to detective," he growled. "I was going to be captain one day — just like Grandad. Just like my uncles after him. You ruined everything. I can't even get a job as a meter maid now. Do you know what that feels like?"

She told herself to stay calm. She was trained to deal with situations like this. Regardless of the fact that she was up against someone with similar training, she was going to have to outsmart him.

He turned the key and the engine roared to life. He hit the gas and the vehicle sped away from the curb.

17

Liam woke up to the sound of his phone ringing. When he glanced at the clock on his bedside table, he saw that it was almost one in the morning.

"What the hell?" he mumbled groggily, reaching for the irritating device. Shaylee was sleeping in the room next door and he didn't want it to wake her up. When he saw Sammy's number flashing on the caller ID, he was suddenly wide awake. Jacy, was his first thought. If Sammy was calling at this hour, something had to have happened to his sister.

"What's wrong?" he asked in greeting, sitting up straight and already preparing to get out of bed.

"I'm sorry to call you so late. I need you to do me a favor."

His gaze narrowed. "Are you serious?"

"Yes, Liam, I'm serious. Mila isn't with you, is she?"

Liam frowned. "No, why?"

"Can you go up to her apartment and see if she's there?"

Liam was on his feet instantly. "What is going on?"

"I'm not sure. I only know she called in a situation, was supposed to meet her supervisor at the station and never showed up. The guy called me and wondered if I knew what was going on with her."

Liam's skin chilled. "What do you mean *a situation*?"

"I can't go into detail with you. Will you just go check?"

Liam grabbed a shirt and pulled it over his head. Then he made his way through his dark apartment, turning lights on along the way. Once he was in the hallway, he glanced through the front door. Mila's SUV wasn't parked in its usual spot. He told Sammy so.

"When was the last time you saw her?"

He grimaced as he thought back to the way they'd parted the morning before. She'd left his apartment without so much as a goodbye. As much as he'd hated the fact, he'd let her go. He really hadn't had any choice. If she wanted time to think, he knew he had to give it to her.

"Are you there?" Sammy demanded.

"I'm here. Yesterday morning was the last time I saw her." He started getting a little worried himself. "She was supposed to meet her supervisor last night?"

"According to him. He said she called and asked him for advice on a victim from a burglary she and Ledbetter dealt with a week or so ago. She was supposed to meet him and the girl at the station. That was hours ago."

"Have you called her brother? Maybe something happened with him."

"I called him. He spoke to her earlier today. She was okay then. He's upset now, too."

Liam squeezed the suddenly tense muscles in the back of his neck. "Something doesn't feel right about this. She wouldn't call the station and tell someone she was coming in if she wasn't planning on showing up—especially after she's walking on such thin ice with Tennant."

"I was thinking the same thing. Listen, I need to go. I've got a call coming in. Let me know if you talk to her."

Liam agreed and hung up. Too keyed up to go back to bed, he stared out into the darkness. He frowned, suddenly feeling a chill.

Grabbing his jacket, he exited the apartment and went upstairs to hers. Just for the hell of it, he knocked. There was the possibility that her car had broken down again and she'd had to Uber back home. She'd mentioned buying a new battery but that didn't mean there weren't other problems with the older model vehicle.

He waited for a few minutes before he gave up and went back downstairs. Walking out into the front yard, he strode toward the parking area. There was a streetlight just to the left of his vehicle that lit things up fairly well. He didn't see anything alarming at first, besides the fact that her SUV wasn't there.

Still, he felt like something wasn't right.

Sighing, he examined the street. The other houses nearby were all dark other than a porch light or two. Everything seemed quiet and peaceful. Ordinary.

He swore and turned to go back into the house. That's when he saw it. The red iPhone lying in the street not far from his truck.

His blood ran cold again and he walked over and bent, taking a look at the device. He recognized it right away. It was Mila's.

Picking it up, he hit the screen with his thumb. There was a picture of her and her brother on the home screen, confirming what he already knew.

Swearing again, he dug his own phone from

his pocket and dialed Sammy's number.

. . .

Mila stayed silent in the seat next to Ledbetter as he drove her SUV to the interstate. He pulled onto the freeway heading south.

"We've got a little time to kill. I didn't expect you to leave your apartment until morning."

She shivered at the idea that he'd been watching her. That explained the odd feeling she'd felt in the hallway when she'd gone after her mail earlier in the evening. "Where are we going?"

"Just for a drive. Sit back and enjoy the scenery."

She struggled to use her training to find a way out the mess she was in. She knew he was growing more and more unstable with every minute that passed. He had a whiskey bottle in his coat pocket and every so often he pulled it out a took a big swig. She had to do something now to change his course. She knew instinctively that when he reached whatever destination he had in mind, more bad things were going to happen.

Taking a deep breath, she looked at him. "Your career isn't over if you re-think what you're doing right now, Bryan. I could put in a good word for you with another department. You could go someplace where nobody knows you and start over. That's what I did."

He snorted. "Yeah, that worked out well for you." He shook his head. "Don't try to be my friend now, *Mila*." He said her first name sarcastically. "I'm not dumb enough to believe you'd ever do anything like that. And even if you would, Tennant's blacklisted me. He already warned me I'll never work in law enforcement again as long as he's around."

She wasn't exactly surprised. Tennant really had no other alternatives after what Ledbetter had done.

"I don't need you and I don't need that asshole, Tennant," he rambled on. "Neither of you are going to be a problem for me much longer." He took an exit and turned off into the hills above the city. He pulled over on an abandoned road and cut the engine. "Make yourself comfortable. We're going to be here for a bit. Feel free to take a nap."

Was he serious?

He was, she realized. Keeping his weapon handy, he leaned back against the door and started humming.

How had this man ever passed the psychological testing required to become a police officer? He was far from sane.

She contemplated every option she had for escape. He was watching her like a hawk. There was no pushing the unlock button. She knew he'd shoot her before her feet hit the ground outside. Her only hope was that the whiskey would do its job and put him to sleep.

Minutes ticked by, then hours. Still, he sat there, staring at her with vacant eyes. It made her skin crawl.

"Why are we just sitting here?" she finally asked, completely unnerved. Nothing he was doing made any sense. Was he planning to kill her? If he was, what was he waiting for?

"You'll know soon enough."

No matter what she said after that, he refused to acknowledge her.

Another two hours went by. Finally, around six in the morning, he started up the SUV again.

Startled at the sudden movement, she straightened. "Where are we going?"

"I told you; you'll know soon enough."

She watched the passing scenery. They were headed back to the interstate. He took the exit toward downtown and turned left. She suddenly realized where he was heading. The precinct was only a few blocks up. He couldn't possibly be taking her there. A very sick feeling washed over her and she forced herself to look his way. "Where are you taking me?"

"I think you've figured that out."

She knew better than to think he was letting her go and turning himself in. Not after all this. "You can't be heading to the precinct. You'll be arrested."

"No," was all he said.

She narrowed her eyes. "What do you mean *no*?" A thought occurred to her out of nowhere as she recalled something he'd said to her earlier. "And what did you mean by Tennant and I not being a problem for you much longer? What are you doing, Bryan? You can't possibly think you're going to take on an entire police precinct."

"No. You are."

"Me?"

"You'll understand everything in about—" He glanced at his watch. "—twenty minutes."

Her skin pebbled at the nonchalant tone to his voice. "What have you done?"

"I keep telling you; it's not me, it's you. *Your* car at the scene. *Your* note sent to the precinct explaining your grievances. *Your* locker the explosive device was left in."

Mila swallowed hard. She wanted to believe he was bluffing but the cold look in his eyes told her otherwise. Her anxiety overflowed and she flew into a full-blown panic. "You couldn't have just walked in there with a bomb without anyone questioning you. You don't even work there anymore."

"I had to clean out my locker, sweetheart. Nobody paid me any attention." He smirked. "When you turn up dead, nobody will so much as shed a tear after what *you've* done."

She continued to shake her head, even though the cop in her told her what he was saying was very possibly true. He'd set her up. He was going to blow up the precinct, killing God knew how many people, and she would be blamed for it.

"You want proof?" He pulled his phone from his pocket and brought up an app. He turned the phone around so she could see a timer running. It had just under fifteen minutes on it.

Her breath caught in her throat and she struggled for air.

Unaffected, he pulled the SUV to a stop about a block from the precinct and shut off the engine. "Now you can see *your* handiwork." He pulled out his whiskey bottle and took a long swig. "I know you hate him, too—Tennant. He demoted you—treated you like a child. He's getting what he deserves."

"I don't hate him," she argued, finally finding her voice. "I was mad at myself for making so many mistakes with my own career. He was only doing his job."

"That may be your truth, but the truth

everyone is going to believe when this is all said and done is that you held a grudge. You were angry and you went after revenge. What better revenge than this?" He let out a chuckle. "I always wondered if all those Saturdays I spent with my uncle would come in handy someday. He's a whiz with explosives. He taught me how to make my own fireworks when I was eight."

She suddenly recalled the conversation she'd had with Brubaker and Jones about Ledbetter's uncle. He'd been a well-respected member of PPB's bomb squad.

She felt a bead of sweat dribble down the side of her face. "You're going to kill innocent people. Don't you realize that? Do you even care?"

"Nobody in that precinct gave a shit about me. So, no, I don't care." He continued staring at the countdown on his phone.

She knew she had to do something — anything to stop him. If she died in the process, so be it. He was going to kill her anyway.

Staring up the street, she watched as the morning shift change took place. She recognized people coming and going. She had no idea who was already in the building. The bastard had picked the busiest time of the day, certainly on purpose. He wanted to kill as many people as he could.

She felt so desperate it was torture. There was no way for her to communicate with anyone. People were far enough away that nobody of any consequence would notice them.

"Accepting your fate, are you?"

She glared at him. "You'll go to hell for this. At least my fate isn't as bad as that."

He didn't bat an eye. "My life has been hell anyway. Living up to the standards of my fucked up family hasn't been Heaven, that's for sure."

She started to shoot back an angry retort when something caught her eye. A very familiar pickup truck pulled up in front of the precinct and parked. She wanted to deny what she was seeing.

Liam. He climbed out of the driver's seat and hopped to the pavement.

Her first instinct was to pound on the window—to scream. Hell, to do anything that would attract any type of attention at all. Nothing worked. It was like she was completely invisible.

"Huh," Ledbetter smirked as he realized who Liam was. "Now this is an added bonus."

She wanted to kill him at that moment. If she'd had a weapon...

He grinned at her.

And that was the straw that broke the camel's

back. She completely lost all sense of reality. Back in the day, when she'd been in the military, she'd gone through some harrowing situations. Once adrenaline took over, rational thought fled. She attacked him with everything she had, her fingers going for his eyes, her knee going straight for his crotch.

He let out a howl and fought back. Fortunately, he lost his grip on the gun he held and it clattered to the floor, out of his reach. She continued to pummel him but he was strong. He slammed her back against the dashboard and she saw stars long enough to wince. Ignoring the pain, she continued to fight. He had her flat against the passenger seat quickly, his fingers wrapped around her neck.

"You fucking bitch! I'm going to kill you!"

Her hand dropped down toward the floor and she felt around, desperately searching for the weapon he'd dropped. She knew it had slid somewhere under the seat.

Lack of oxygen had her weakening. She began to see spots. She told herself not to give in to the impending darkness. She had to keep fighting.

As if God himself came down and helped her forge on, her fingers connected with something metallic and cold underneath the seat. She gripped the weapon, just as Ledbetter tightened his fingers around her neck and gave a rough squeeze.

The shot went off abruptly and she didn't even see a reaction in his eyes as the bullet hit him. He just dropped like a ton of bricks, landing with a thump on top of her.

It took a moment for her to realize she was free. As she gulped in air, she struggled to move from underneath him. Her only thought was that she had to get into the precinct and warn everyone. She knew the timer had to be ticking down to its last minutes.

Using every ounce of strength she had, she hit the lock button and managed to open the car door. It took some work, but she was eventually able to back herself out onto the pavement. Standing up quickly, she held onto the car door, desperate to steady herself. A wave of dizziness nearly took her to the ground again.

She didn't give herself a chance to contemplate things. She took off down the street toward the precinct, screaming the entire way.

She hit the doors to the lobby and immediately gained the attention of Finley Jones. After that, everything moved in slow motion. Finley was able to make sense of what she was saying and immediately called for the building to be evacuated.

As people rushed by, Mila kept her eyes open

for Liam, for Sammy or Slade or Tennant. She didn't see any of them. Panic continued to bubble over and she tried to head for the back of the building. Someone grabbed her and yanked her in the other direction. Brubaker, she realized.

"Liam Colson. He was in here. Where is he?" she asked frantically.

"I don't know, Barnes. There were people in back of the building. They probably went out the other door."

Before he could stop her, she took off in that direction. There was no way she was leaving until she knew Liam was safe. For his daughter's sake, she had to be sure he was okay.

. . .

The crowd that conglomerated out on the street about a block from the precinct thickened with every minute that passed. Liam watched carefully, looking for any sign of Mila. He'd heard about what she'd done—storming the precinct, screaming about a bomb. Everyone had evacuated and he'd been watching for her— knowing she had to be in the crowd somewhere.

"Where is she?" he asked Sammy, who stood nearby.

"Probably out front. I'm sure she's safe. With

all these people from the nearby businesses, you'll never find her."

Liam had a very uneasy feeling and grimaced. Suddenly he saw Carter Brubaker heading his way.

"Is Barnes with you?" Carter asked breathlessly.

Liam's heart took a dive and he shook his head.

"She was looking for you. I tried to get her outside when I left but she refused to leave without you." Carter bent over at the knees, breathing hard.

Liam didn't think at all, he just took off in a sprint toward the building. He heard Sammy behind him, yelling. He ignored his friend.

Just as he rounded the corner, he saw the van holding the bomb squad arrive on the scene.

He didn't let that stop him. He went straight for the front doors of the precinct, despite the warnings he heard from people nearby. Blocking out the sound of approaching sirens, he whipped one open. That's when he saw Mila. She was running toward him. Her entire upper body was covered with blood.

Panicked, he grabbed her by the arm. He didn't get one word out before she was screaming at him to run. He could see by the terrified look on her face she was deadly serious.

He turned, dragging her with him.   They both took off in a sprint.   Just as they reached the street, an explosion sounded from behind them. They were both lifted off their feet. He kept his arms around her as they landed hard on the pavement. He did his best to shield both their heads from flying debris and said a silent prayer.

18

Mila fidgeted uneasily. Captain Tennant sat across from her, behind his desk. As was getting to be the norm for her, he was frowning at her.

It had been three weeks since the incident with Bryan Ledbetter—three weeks since the bomb he'd rigged had blown up a good portion of Precinct 124.

Nobody had been killed that day, aside from Ledbetter himself—who had died as a result of the gunshot wound Mila had inflicted on him in self-defense.

The building had been extensively damaged and was currently under repair so staff was currently using space in a nearby property owned by the city.

Mila hadn't been on the job since the incident. She was still on administrative leave. She was following protocol and seeing a psychologist recommended by the department. It was helping her deal with things. While she'd disliked Ledbetter and he'd turned out to be a very sick individual, the fact that she'd been forced to kill him weighed heavily on her mind. At night, he was still haunting her nightmares. She supposed he probably always would.

"You look better, Barnes. How do you feel?"

"Fine, sir," she replied automatically.

"That's bullshit. Tell me the truth."

Tennant was far too intuitive. "I'm better. Ready to get back to work." The answer was about as honest as she was going to get with him.

"There's no rush. Psyche says you need more time."

She refrained from grumbling. She knew there was no point.

"Look, I realize it's hard being on the sidelines. It's for your own good. But I wanted to let you know, we made an arrest in the Whitfield case. That sketch we put out led us straight to the perp. Guy had plenty of priors. He won't be getting out of jail anytime soon. Good job on your instincts with that one. That girl will sleep a whole lot better knowing her attacker is locked up."

Mila knew that was true. She'd actually spoken to Jana herself a few days ago. The teenager was getting help to deal with her own trauma but she, too, was on the road to recovery.

"We'll revisit your situation in another week. Use the resources the department's offering you. Call me if you need anything."

Sensing her dismissal, Mila stood and exited the office. She ran into Sammy in the hallway. He was headed for the exit, too, so they walked together.

"Still not cleared?" he questioned, a sympathetic smile on his face.

"Another week," was all she said.

"Probably best not to rush back."

"So you'd want to be stuck at home, staring at soap operas and bad talk shows all day?"

He winced. "No."

"That's what I thought." She hit her key fob as they reached her vehicle. Leaning back against the driver's side door, she considered him. "How's Liam?"

He arched a brow. "He's good. Any reason you're avoiding asking him yourself?"

She bit her bottom lip, a pang stabbing her in the heart. She'd only seen Liam once since the day of the bombing. They'd passed in the hallway outside their apartments. The conversation had been guarded but polite. In other words, awkward.

"He's a good guy, Mila. I wouldn't steer you wrong there. It's pretty obvious you guys like each other so what's the problem?"

"You seemed a little less positive about us the last time we talked about it," she reminded him cautiously.

He shrugged. "The day that bomb went off, a lot of things came into perspective for me. I saw the way you two were looking at each other. You're in denial. Why screw around wasting time when it's obvious you've got something between you?"

She thought about that. "Because it's not just the two of us."

He folded his arms over his chest. "People divorce all the time. The kids are important but they don't mean that a person can't find love again—maybe the *right* love the second time around."

She found her lips quirking. "For a big, tough cop, that was pretty poetic."

He snorted. "Call it what you want. It's been weeks. I think you've had plenty of time to think about things. If you weren't still into him, we wouldn't be having this conversation right now. Give him a chance."

She watched him walk away, wishing things were as easy as he made them so sound.

Sliding into her vehicle, she started it up and drove toward home. The entire way, she tried to tell herself she didn't miss being with Liam. She tried to tell herself she didn't miss Shaylee.

But she did. She missed them both. A lot.

By the time she parked in front of the Victorian, she realized Sammy was right. She had feelings for Liam and they weren't going away. He'd left the ball in her court. Maybe it was time she picked the damn thing up and ran with it.

. . .

Liam leaned back on his couch, a beer in his hand.

Travis sat nearby, nursing his own beverage.

The past few weeks had been long. He hadn't sustained any physical injuries from the bombing at the police precinct but recovering mentally had been a little challenging. He'd cheated death, yet again. He'd done so on the job various times and sometimes he found himself counting to see how close he was to hitting his nine lives.

"Have you talked to her?"

Liam met his friend's gaze. "Who?"

Travis rolled his eyes. "Who do you think?"

Realizing he meant Mila, Liam shrugged.

"No."

"Why not?"

"Because that's the way she wants it."

"Says who?"

Liam scowled. "I told you I left things up to her. She's got a lot in her life to deal with right now. After what happened…" He grimaced as he thought about Ledbetter and what Mila had gone through. "Her situation's pretty complicated."

Travis took a swig of beer. "Okay. Fair enough, I guess." He straightened. "I've been meaning to talk to you about something. It's about Sloan."

"What about her?" Liam had been so wrapped up in his own business lately, he hadn't seen Sloan in a while—or her husband, for that matter.

Travis hesitated. "I probably shouldn't talk to you about this but…" He leaned over, setting his beer bottle on the coffee table. "She and Justin have been trying to have a baby for over a year now. They got tested and all that. Apparently he's the problem. He's sterile."

Liam winced. "That sucks."

"Yeah." Travis blew out a breath.

Liam could see tension in his friend's normally nonchalant gaze. "I'm sorry. I know you and Sloan are tight. There's always adoption."

Travis dangled his hands between his knees. "I mentioned that to her. She's been looking into IUI—Intrauterine Insemination."

Liam thought that over. "Like using a sperm doner?"

Travis nodded.

Liam could tell Travis was leaving something out. "Why do you look so stressed? People do that stuff all the time. If   Justin can't have a kid—"

"She asked for mine."

Liam's eyes grew wide. "Say that again."

Travis met Liam's gaze. "She asked for *mine*."

Liam set his own beer aside. "Your *sperm*?"

Travis nodded silently.

Liam muttered an oath. "What did you tell her?"

"I didn't tell her anything. I sat there pretty much like you are right now."

"Wow."

"Yeah, wow." Travis flopped back against the cushions. "I love her. You know that. We've been best friends since we were kids. But this…" He shook his head and raked a hand through his hair. "Shit. I just don't know."

"What does Justin think about it?"

"He's onboard, I guess. I'm not tight with him like I am with Sloan but she said he agreed to it."

"Wow," Liam repeated.

"Stop saying that."

"I don't know what else to say."

"If you were me, what would you do?"

Liam didn't answer right away. "I don't know, dude. I mean I have Shaylee so I guess for me, I can't imagine someone else raising my kid. You know what I've gone through with Shelby and Pam."

"Yeah, I've thought about that." Travis scraped a hand over his jaw. "I've literally been lying awake every night thinking about this. It's driving me crazy. She hasn't called me since. I think she's just waiting me out."

Liam didn't envy his friend, that was for sure. "So say you did it. How do you go about things? I mean would you have to...?" His words trailed off. "You know..."

"No!" Travis replied automatically. "It's all very technical. I give them a...sample." He visibly stiffened. "The doctor takes it from there. I'm not involved in any other way."

"Except you are," Liam pointed out.

"Yeah. Exactly."

"There are a lot of doners out there. Why you?"

"She doesn't want someone random. I think they're just going to give up on the whole thing if this doesn't work out."

"That's a lot of pressure on you."

"Tell me about it." Travis sighed and took another long swig of his beer. "I don't know why I'm even considering it. It's insane. There's no way I can see the kid and treat it like it's not mine. It would be my flesh and blood."

Liam couldn't argue. "I guess you have your answer then."

"Only I don't. I just keep seeing Sloan's face. She was so desperate. I know how much she loves kids. And they've been trying for so long."

"Nobody would blame you for saying no, Trav. In fact, I think most men in your position would, best friend or not."

Travis remained silent.

A knock interrupted the awkward moment.

Liam went to the door and opened it. He was surprised to find Mila standing in the hallway. He stared at her curiously.

"Is this a bad time?" She met his gaze questioningly.

"No. I was just leaving," Travis appeared out of nowhere and gave Liam an encouraging nod. He smiled in Mila's direction. "How's it going?"

She smiled back awkwardly as she stepped out of his way. "Good. You don't have to take off on my account. I can come back later."

"I've got stuff to do. No worries." Travis was gone before Liam could stop him.

"I'm sorry. I should have called first."

Liam opened the door wider. "It's not a big deal. We were just having a beer. You want one?"

She shook her head. "Not really. I owe you an apology."

He wasn't sure what she was apologizing for so he just stood there and waited for more.

"I have feelings for you, Liam. Real feelings. They scare me. I'm not good with relationships and I don't know a lot about kids." She paused. "The past few weeks, I've done a lot of thinking. I've kept to myself, hoping I would just get over this thing with us. But I haven't. I miss seeing you — miss seeing Shaylee. I know we've had a lot of complications and chaos, but I thought maybe we could start over."

He leaned against the doorjamb. They just stared at each other for a long time. He realized right then he had some pretty serious feelings for her, too. And he'd missed her like crazy. "I'm not so good with relationships, either. It's going to be like the blind leading the blind."

Her lips quirked. "Maybe that's a good thing. Neither one of us is going to have unreasonable expectations."

She had a point.

Straightening, he reached for her, his hands wrapping around her waist. He lowered his head and rubbed his nose against hers softly. "I think I might have a loaf of cheese and some crackers inside. You hungry?"

She grinned as his mouth covered hers. "I'm always hungry. But I think the crackers and cheese can wait."

. . .

Travis stared at his phone, his finger hovering over her number.

Sloan Wyatt. His best friend in the world. He honestly couldn't remember a time in his life when the tiny, brunette fireball hadn't been part of it.

They'd met on the playground in second grade. His friend at the time had pushed her off the slide and attempted to bully her into giving him her lunch money. Before Travis had been able to step in and right the situation, Sloan had bloodied the creep's nose and damn near taken his lunch money instead.

From that point on, she and Travis had been inseparable. When her first boyfriend had broken her heart in junior high, Travis had kicked the guy's ass. When she hadn't made cheerleading in high school, he'd been the one to dry her tears. In college, when she'd been homesick and desperate to quit after only a few weeks, he'd shown up and set her straight. She'd ended up graduating Summa Cum Laude.

Shortly after that, he'd gotten married. She'd been there, as his "best man" and held the rings for him. When the marriage had fallen apart a few short years later, she'd helped him pick up the pieces.

That was just how their relationship was. They were each other's rocks.

But now, he was facing a very tough decision.

Could he really stand in the way of her dream to have a baby?

It was a lot of anyone to ask, he reminded himself.

But she wasn't just *anyone*.

He stared at his phone again. Eventually, biting the bullet, he hit her number. The phone rang twice before she answered.

"Are you mad at me?" she asked in greeting. "Because I wouldn't blame you if you were. I don't know what I was thinking, putting you on the spot like that. It was out of line and —"

"Okay," he interrupted her, even surprising himself a little.

Dead silence followed.

"What did you say?" she eventually asked.

He exhaled deeply. "I said, okay. I'll do it."

**LOOK FOR TRAVIS'S STORY
HALF PAST MIDNIGHT
(BOOK 6 in the PORTLAND 911 SERIES)
COMING SOON!**

AVAILABLE TITLES BY JENNIFER HAYDEN

HIDE AND SEEK
(Book 1 Hide and Seek Mystery Series)
UNBROKEN
(Book 2 Hide and Seek Mystery Series)
COLLISION
(Book 3 Hide and Seek Mystery Series)
SWEET REVENGE
SAY MERCY
SOUNDS OF NIGHT
ROOT OF ALL EVIL
AFTER THE RAIN
(Book 1 – The Callahans)
IN THE EYE OF THE STORM
(Book 2 – The Callahans)
AFTERSHOCK
(Book 3 – The Callahans)
LESS THAN PERFECT
(Book 4 - The Callahans)
DESERT HEAT
(Book 5 – The Callahans)
SHATTERED
(Book 6 – The Callahans)
HOPE FOR CHRISTMAS
(Book 1 in Noel, Montana)
HEAD OVER HEELS FOR CHRISTMAS

SMOKESCREEN

(Book 2 in Noel, Montana)
SKELETONS IN THE MIST
(The McCalls – Book 1)
BENEATH BURIED SECRETS
(The McCalls – Book 2)
FATAL VOWS
(The McCalls – Book 3)
HIDDEN MEMORIES
SHAMELESS
ON THIN ICE
MERMAID COVE
(Mermaid Cove - Book 1)
RED TIDE
(Mermaid Cove - Book 2)
BREAKWATER
(Mermaid Cove - Book 3)
MAYHEM AND MISTLETOE
(Mermaid Cove - Book 4)
HIDEAWAY HALL
LOCKDOWN
IN CREPT EVIL
CAUGHT IN THE MIDDLE
(Seattle 911 – Book 1)
TWIST OF FATE
(Seattle 911 – Book 2)
HINDSIGHT
(Seattle 911 – Book 3)
DEAD SILENCE
(Seattle 911 – Book 4)
IN PLAIN SIGHT

(Seattle 911 – Book 5)
DIRTY LITTLE SECRETS
(Seattle 911 – Book 6)
DANGEROUS LIES
(Seattle 911 – Book 7)
BLACKOUT
(Seattle 911 – Book 8)
UNFORGIVEN
(Seattle 911 – Book 9)
BACKFIRE
(Seattle 911 – Book 10)
HAUNTED
(Seattle 911 – Book 11)
JUST WHISPER
(Seattle 911 – Book 12)
BEFORE DAWN
(Seattle 911 – Book 13)
BAD BLOOD
(Seattle 911 – Book 14)
THE RECKONING
SEE NO EVIL
(The Meadows – Book 1)
HEAR NO EVIL
(The Meadows – Book 2)
SPEAK NO EVIL
(The Meadows – Book 3)
LIES THAT BIND
(The Lennox Sisters – Book 1)
COLD TO THE BONE
(The Lennox Sisters – Book 2)

STOLEN
(Portland 911 – Book 1)
BETRAYED
(Portland 911 – Book 2)
SOLE SURVIVOR
(Portland 911 – Book 3)
WILDFIRE
(Portland 911 – Book 4)
SMOKESCREEN
(Portland 911 – Book 5)

WWW.JENNIFERHAYDENBOOKS.COM